P9-CEI-689

"You're trouble, Karen."

The lean body was tensed, his features set in lines that boded ill. When Jake spoke, it was in low but far from soft tones. "I'm going to take a great deal of pleasure in putting you where you belong."

Karen widened her eyes at him provocatively, sure of her safety with the others well within yelling distance. "It takes two, Professor. I doubt if your reputation would be enhanced by any suggestion of rape in the backwoods."

"_____," he asked, "said anything about rape? _ were ready enough to go along last night."

The flush started deep; she was thankful of the dim lighting to conceal it from him. "A combination of too much wine and not enough sleep," she claimed. "You wouldn't find me as receptive again."

KAY THORPE, an English author, has always been able to spin a good yarn. In fact, her teachers said she was the best storyteller in the school—particularly with excuses for being late! Kay then explored a few unsatisfactory career paths before giving rein to her imagination and hitting the jackpot with her first romance novel. After a roundabout route, she'd found her niche at last. The author is married with one son.

Books by Kay Thorpe

Don't miss any of our special offers. Write to us at the following address for information on our newest releases.

Harlequin Reader Service
P.O. Box 1397, Buffalo, NY 14240
Canadian address: P.O. Box 603,
Fort Erie, Ont. L2A 5X3

KAY THORPE

Wild Streak

Harlequin Books

TORONTO • NEW YORK • LONDON
AMSTERDAM • PARIS • SYDNEY • HAMBURG
STOCKHOLM • ATHENS • TOKYO • MILAN
MADRID • WARSAW • BUDAPEST • AUCKLAND

If you purchased this book without a cover you should be aware
that this book is stolen property. It was reported as "unsold and
destroyed" to the publisher, and neither the author nor the
publisher has received any payment for this "stripped book."

Harlequin Presents first edition May 1993
ISBN 0-373-11556-3

Original hardcover edition published in 1991
by Mills & Boon Limited

WILD STREAK

Copyright © 1991 by Kay Thorpe. All rights reserved.
Except for use in any review, the reproduction or utilization
of this work in whole or in part in any form by any electronic,
mechanical or other means, now known or hereafter invented,
including xerography, photocopying and recording,
or in any information storage or retrieval system, is forbidden without
the permission of the publisher, Harlequin Enterprises Limited,
225 Duncan Mill Road, Don Mills, Ontario, Canada M3B 3K9.

All the characters in this book have no existence outside the
imagination of the author and have no relation whatsoever to
anyone bearing the same name or names. They are not even
distantly inspired by any individual known or unknown to the
author, and all incidents are pure invention.

® are Trademarks registered in the United States Patent and
Trademark Office and in other countries.

Printed in U.S.A.

CHAPTER ONE

IN THE falling dusk, glowing rivers of lava could be seen pouring down the flanks of Pacaya more than twenty miles away. Just one of the eight active volcanoes right here in Guatemala alone, Karen reflected, wondering how people could live with such ever-present danger. At least her own stay in the country was of a temporary nature.

'There are no volcanoes where we're going,' said the fair-haired man seated at her side in the rear of the taxi-cab, accurately guessing her thoughts. 'Petan is mostly lowland jungle country. It's going to be hellishly hot and sticky. Think you'll be up to it?'

Karen turned her head to smile at him, eyes reflecting the passing lights from other vehicles on the highway. 'It's a bit late to start having doubts now.'

Roger Halsey returned the smile. 'I'm not having doubts; I simply wondered if you were.'

'Not likely! This is just the kind of thing I hoped for when I applied for the job.'

'Just asking,' he came back equably. 'I didn't really anticipate any other reply. You wouldn't be here at all if I'd thought there was any chance of you letting me down.' He studied her for a moment, taking in the pure oval of her face with its high cheekbones and brilliant green eyes, the inward curve of naturally blonde hair. His expression underwent a subtle alteration. 'You should be in front of the camera, not behind it, looking the way you do.'

'Except that I can't act for toffee,' Karen responded without regret. 'I'm more than happy to be where I am. Looks don't come into it. You said Professor Rothman came in a couple of days ago?'

'That's right. He's borrowed the house we're going to be using as a base while we're in the city from a friend who's out of the country at present. He covered some of the same territory a year or so back, using the same guide we'll be using this time.' His voice took on enthusiasm. 'It was a brilliant idea of his to take the viewers with him on this expedition. We're going to get some superb footage.'

'With Jake Rothman taking all the credit as usual,' cut in Karen drily. 'Doesn't anyone out there ever realise that it's the production that counts? Without you and the cameras, he's just another archaeologist.'

'Rather more than that. His interests extend to most branches of natural science too. Anyway, his is the name that sells the end product. I have the satisfaction of knowing mine counts with those who matter when it comes down to allocations. Jake's OK to work with, and he knows his stuff backwards. He's only in his mid-thirties, which makes him something pretty special in his field.'

'I gather he isn't married.'

'No.' The good-looking features acquired an ironic expression. 'He's waiting for the right woman.'

Karen gave him a swift, sympathetic glance. Her boss's marital problems were no secret. At thirty-two, he was one of the top documentary producer-directors in the business, which hardly made for a settled home-life. As his assistant, she had seen little of her own home these past few months.

She had applied for the job without much hope. Coming from the relative obscurity of a provincial television station, she had known herself sadly lacking in the kind of experience required by the major league. Roger had given her the biggest boost of her whole twenty-four years in offering her the post. And now here she was, accompanying him on what promised to be the experience of a lifetime. Could anyone ask for more?

'I still can't believe I'm really doing this,' she said. 'I only hope I don't let the team down.'

Roger smiled. 'You won't do that either. You're the best assistant I've ever had.'

Karen warmed to the compliment. 'Thanks,' she said softly. She turned to glance out of the rear window at the following traffic. 'We seem to have lost the other cab.'

'Howard has the address,' returned Roger without concern. 'He'll be making sure the driver doesn't put his camera at risk. Lives are secondary. We should be there soon.'

As if in direct answer to the comment, their driver left the highway to take a left-hand turn down a narrow side-street, followed by another and yet another until drawing finally to a halt before double wooden gates set into a high stone wall.

'I'd say we've arrived,' said Roger. 'Hop out and ring the bell up there, will you, while I see to the bags and settle up?'

Karen got out of the taxi, stretching limbs still stiff from the long flight. Her skirt had ridden up. She pulled it down to its rightful position just above her knees before moving to reach for the bell-pull set to one side of the doors. The deep clang was loud enough to waken the dead, yet no one had come to open the door by the time the taxi drove away.

'Try it again,' advised Roger. 'There has to be someone around.'

The second pull brought almost immediate response. Grumbling under his breath in Spanish, the man who admitted them took care to close both doors again before indicating that they should accompany him, ignoring Karen's observation that the rest of the party would be here any moment.

The courtyard fronting the house was full of colour from the passion flower vines climbing everywhere. Brilliant blues, rich crimsons and yellows dazzled the eye. The house itself was Spanish in design, with fretted ironwork at the windows, and an arched balcony running around at first-floor level.

A flight of stone steps led up and into this. A man came out through opened glass doors as they reached the top, his expression undergoing a sudden and disconcerting alteration as a pair of penetrating blue eyes came to rest on Karen.

'There was nothing said about having a woman along,' he clipped.

Bridling at the tone, Karen gave him back look for look. 'Is that a problem, Professor Rothman?'

The angular, intelligent features failed to relax. 'Not if I have anything to do with it. Who are you, anyway?'

'Karen Lewis,' supplied Roger before she could answer. 'My assistant.' He held out a hand. 'Good to see you, Jake.'

'You too.' The other man added shortly, 'Afraid I can't say the same about your choice of assistant.'

'I'm here because I happen to be very good at my job,' Karen answered, keeping a tight rein on her temper.

'I was under the impression that that was what counted these days.'

'In some spheres, maybe.' Jake Rothman looked anything but sympathetic. 'Where we're going there's no room for the equal-rights brigade to set up shop. You'd never stand the pace.'

Facing up to him, Karen was aware of his height and fit, lean build, of the sheer hard-boned masculinity of his features. The only incongruity was in the thick dark hair, which showed a distinct tendency to curl at the ends, despite the ruthlessness of its cut. She had watched his two previous productions on TV, but meeting the man in person was something else again. Not one to be taken lightly.

'Try me,' she challenged, and saw the blue eyes take on a sudden ironic glint.

'An invitation I'll have to turn down, I'm afraid. However, there's no reason why you shouldn't stick around until we leave for Petan. You're decidedly easy on the eye.'

'Easy to see you have only one use for women,' she retorted incautiously. 'I've met men like you before!'

'And handled them with equal ease, I'm sure.' The sarcasm was muted, his amusement plain. 'Do come in, Miss Lewis. You too, Roger. You must be ready for a drink.'

'Gasping.' The younger man was obviously not about to labour the point right away, although the glance he sent Karen's way was reassuring. Let it lie for the moment, was what he appeared to be intimating.

Fuming, she stalked ahead of both men into the spacious room beyond the doors. Furnished in dark wood, with bright covers and drapes, it was a cross between old and new Spanish; comfortable rather than luxurious. Plant life spilled in profusion from every available surface. At any other time, Karen could have appreciated the welcoming ambience of the place. Right now she was incapable of appreciating anything.

'I'll have Manuel see to a room for you,' said Jake. 'In the meantime, you might like to join us in a drink?'

Karen bit back the sarcastic comment. This was no time to indulge in that kind of repartee. 'Thanks,' she said levelly. 'I'll have a vodka on the rocks, please.'

Dark brows lifted. 'Trying to prove something?'

'Only that I like vodka.' She took a seat on one of the sofas, about to cross her legs, when she realised that Roger, sitting opposite, would have a fine view of her upper limbs if she did so. She should have worn trousers, she thought irritably. Short skirts might be fashionable, but they loaned the wrong image. Had she arrived without make-up and dressed like a man, Jake Rothman might have taken her a little more seriously.

A forlorn hope, came the immediate rider. Men like Jake Rothman were too hidebound in their prejudices to be swayed by mere trappings. He saw women as the weaker sex all the way through. So it was going to be up to her to prove him wrong. Roger's had to be the final word on whether or not she accompanied the team, of course. As producer, he surely carried the weight? He would no doubt choose his moment to make that clear.

Her drink, when it came, was over-large and of a brand of vodka which must have been almost a hundred per cent proof to judge from the bite in that first swallow. Stifling with an effort the urge to cough and choke, she nodded approval to the man watching her with such infuriating derision. 'Fine, thanks.'

'Obviously an asbestos-lined throat,' he commented drily. 'I've known that stuff knock a hardened drinker for six before now.'

'Which just goes to show I can take the rough as well as the smooth,' she responded, and saw a faint light of appreciation dawn momentarily in the blue eyes.

'Snappy with it too,' he said. 'A pity it's wasted.'

'Perhaps we could talk about this later,' suggested Roger. 'The others should be here any time. They were supposedly right behind us.'

The deep tone of the bell underlined the comment. Jake deposited his own glass on a table and made for the outer door. Not above doing the servant's work when said individual was busy elsewhere, Karen gathered, and felt some faint element of approval infiltrate the antipathy. If the man weren't quite so obnoxious in other attitudes he might have something going for him.

'Sorry about that,' proffered Roger as soon as the other was out of earshot. 'Don't worry about it. I'll straighten things out.'

'When?' she asked.

'As soon as I can get a few minutes with him alone. Once he realises that you're capable of keeping up with the men, he'll come round to the idea.'

'And if he doesn't?'

Roger shrugged and shook his head. 'I need you. That's the bottom line. He has to accept it.'

For the moment she had to be content with that, Karen acknowledged wryly, although she would have preferred an instant confrontation. Jake Rothman had taken the fine edge off her enthusiasm. No matter what, she would always be aware of his antipathy.

'Does he have something against women in general?' she queried after a moment or two.

'Not on the surface. He doesn't exactly go short of female company.'

'But no serious liaisons?'

'None that I know of.' Roger cocked an eyebrow, an odd expression in his eyes. 'Interested that way yourself?'

'Hardly.' She was hard put to it not to over-emphasise the denial. 'You'd think with his background he'd have the intelligence to keep an open mind.'

Roger shrugged again. 'Some men will never see women as their equals.'

'Unlike you.' Her voice had softened. 'It's appreci-ated, Roger, believe me. Your wife doesn't know how lucky she is.'

'My wife,' he said drily, 'takes advantage of the fact.' He hesitated before adding, 'I'm considering divorce as the only solution left. I've tried everything else.'

'Does she know?'

'We haven't sat down and discussed it, if that's what you mean, but I've dropped enough hints. The problem might be getting hold of the evidence I'd need. She's an expert at covering her tracks.'

Karen said quietly, 'You're quite sure she's seeing another man?'

The laugh came harshly. 'The latest in a whole line. I'd have ended it a long time ago if it hadn't been for James.'

'He's still barely five.'

'I know. There seemed a good chance when he was born of making a go of it, only the lull didn't last very long. Fear of losing him is the only thing holding me back.' His eyes came to rest on her face. 'I should have married someone like you.'

Footsteps and voices outside gave her no time to for-mulate a reply. Not that there was very much she could have said, anyway. It had been an off-the-cuff remark, taken no more seriously than he had meant it to be taken. There was nothing of that nature between them.

The three newcomers were loaded down with equipment. Jake Rothman suggested they leave it outside on the balcony for the time being, and settled them down with a drink apiece.

'We'll eat in an hour or so,' he said. 'Give you all a chance to freshen up. There are only three bedrooms, so it means doubling up.' Blue eyes sought green with sardonic intent. 'Apart from Miss Lewis, of course.'

'You don't have to make any special arrangements for me,' Karen protested. 'I'll sleep anywhere.'

Dark brows lifted. 'Maybe you'd care to share my room?' The irony increased at her lack of response. 'No? Well, you might be wise at that. I'll use a roll-away in here. It's only going to be for a couple of nights.' He added to the room in general, 'Miss Lewis won't be coming to Petan.'

Mike Preston, the sound engineer, opened his mouth as if to say something, then shut it again at a shake of the head from Roger. He gave Karen a wink as if in assurance of his support. Some four years or so older than she was herself, he had already made it abundantly clear that he found her irresistibly attractive—an attraction in no way reciprocated. With his carefully styled, blond-tipped hair, jaunty moustache and single figure hip-line, he did nothing at all to her pulse rate. The problem lay in getting him to appreciate that fact. She could only hope that he would keep whatever feelings he might have on the subject of her inclusion in the party to himself. A hint of any personal interest would give Jake Rothman even more ammunition against her.

In his mid-forties, the cameraman, Howard Baxter, was another matter. A quiet man with thinning hair and weathered face, he had worked with Roger on other outside productions over the last three years. They understood one another. Coming over on the plane, Karen had found Howard difficult to reach. Catching his eye now, she found herself wondering if he too disapproved of her presence here. Not that Roger would allow that to make any difference, of course, but having two against her wasn't going to make life any easier.

Howard's assistant, Nigel Morris, hardly counted. Brown-haired, brown-eyed and possessed of scrubbed boyish looks which belied his twenty-six years, he gave the impression of being interested only in his job. At present he was studying the contents of his glass as if his life depended on it.

Conversation centred around the coming project over the next fifteen minutes or so. Karen stayed out of it, unwilling to force Roger into any stand with the others present. Of all the faces in the room, it was Jake's to which her attention kept returning, regardless of every effort to stop herself. His skin was dark from exposure to the elements, though not roughened like Howard's, the bone-structure beneath well defined. The strong jawline showed faint signs of needing a shave.

Catching his eye at one point, she felt her own skin warm, and had to force herself not to look too hastily away. There was no denying the man's male magnetism; it exuded from every pore. If only he weren't quite so objectionable.

It was Jake who finally made a move to break up the party with a glance at his watch.

'Time we started thinking about dinner,' he said. 'Roger, you're in with Howard now, Mike and Nigel together. Which just leaves Miss Lewis.'

'Oh, cut it out,' she said wearily. 'Me Karen, you Jake.'

Surprisingly his lips twitched. 'All right, Karen, supposing I show you your room?'

'You mean *your* room, don't you?' She came to her feet, this time holding the blue gaze without a flicker. 'Lead on.'

The bedrooms were at the rear of the house, one either side of the communal bathroom, the other round the corner along another short length of corridor.

'There's a shower-room attached,' Jake supplied from the doorway as Karen studied the purely masculine abode with its modern divan and navy blue and gold colour scheme. 'Sorry about the lack of frills. Like myself, the owner prefers his life uncluttered.'

Standing with one hand resting lightly on the jamb, he was almost as tall as the doorway itself. Six feet three if he was an inch, Karen judged. Lean-hipped too, but in a manner far different from Mike's whipcord build. His shoulders were certainly broad enough: she could sense the latent power in him. Something stirred to life in the lower half of her abdomen.

'Me too,' she responded, and was aware of a sudden tension in her voice.

One brow rose. 'Does that mean you're unattached?'

'It means,' she said, 'that I like my life uncluttered. If nothing else, we have that much in common.'

He shook his head, mouth sardonic. 'I doubt if we're talking about the same thing. We eat in half an hour.'

'I'm coming with you,' she declared stonily as he began to turn away, unable to contain her resentment any longer. 'I can not only handle the job I've been brought

out here to do, but anything else thrown at me into the
bargain. That includes rough going, be it physical *or*
simple bigotry! I didn't travel five thousand miles to be
rejected on the strength of one man's opinion. If Roger
considers me fit for the job, that's all that matters.'

'And that's not just one man's opinion?' He didn't
bother waiting for an answer.

Biting her lip, Karen acknowledged temporary defeat.
It was down to Roger now. When all was said and done,
he was the one with control of the budget.

The shower proved modern and efficient. Wrapped in
one of the thick white towels, she riffled through her
suitcase to find the cream silk trousers and matching top
she had slipped in at the last moment on the off chance
that she might just have need of something a little more
dressy than the cotton jeans and T-shirts which consti-
tuted the major part of her travelling wardrobe.

That she would be using the latter she couldn't afford
to doubt. The job itself hadn't been a certainty, but she
had won through. She would do the same with Professor
high and mighty Rothman, one way or another.

She found Jake alone in the living-room when she went
through. He was still wearing the same casual trousers
and shirt in which he had greeted them. The glance he
ran over her was deceptively lazy.

'First time I ever knew a woman to be early,' he
commented.

'There's a first time for everything,' Karen returned
with an equability she was far from feeling. 'I didn't
have to share a bathroom, which helped.'

'No, it only occurred to me after I left you that all
my things were still in there.' He ran a hand over a
smooth jawline. 'I borrowed Roger's razor.'

'Who are you out to impress?' she asked sweetly. 'If you'd given me a call I'd have tossed some trousers and a shirt out to you.'

'If I'd been that concerned I'd have come in and fetched them,' came the smooth response. 'If you'll forgive the criticism, you're a bit over-dressed for the occasion yourself. Were you expecting to wear that *en route*?'

'Naturally not.' Karen made every effort to keep the tartness to a minimum. 'I was under the impression that Guatemala City was fairly civilised, that's all. It seemed appropriate to make some concession. The rest of my stuff is extremely practical.'

'Pity you won't be needing it.' The easiness of his stance was belied by the hint of steel in his voice. 'If we can't get you on a flight Friday, you're welcome to stay on here until there's a seat available.'

Karen felt her teeth come together. 'Thanks for the offer, but it won't be necessary. I'm coming with you the whole way, and you're not going to stop me!'

'Think not?' The words were soft but not gentle. 'I'd be interested to hear how you propose to persuade me.'

'I don't need to do any persuading. Roger has overall control of the party.'

'Only where it comes to the actual filming. You'd be a liability.'

'Simply because I'm a woman?' She was too beside herself with anger to heed her vow to let Roger handle things. 'Let me tell you a few facts of life, Professor Rothman. We may be built differently, but there's very little a man can do that we can't! I'm an experienced trekker, for one thing. I've spent many weekends and holidays in the Scottish Highlands and Lake District, covering up to twenty-five miles a day. I'm as fit as you—

fitter, probably, because I'm a good ten years younger—
and I'd match you step for step in whatever kind of
terrain we might meet with!'

She paused there for breath, chest heaving as though
she had been running fast. Jake allowed his gaze to rest
for a lengthy, purposeful moment on the rise and fall of
her breasts beneath the thin material before lifting his
gaze to her face. Karen could feel the warmth running
under her skin.

'How about the other aspect?' he enquired with silky
inflection. 'One woman, five men?'

'*What* about it?' she challenged.

His lips slanted. 'I shouldn't need to spell it out for
you. We're going to be out there some time. Given the
circumstances, any female would present a problem.
Looking the way you do, the problem becomes mag-
nified a hundredfold.'

Her snort was meant to deride. 'You may be incapable of going a few weeks without a woman,
Professor, but don't tar everyone with the same brush.
This is a professional team we're talking about, not an
uncivilised rabble!'

The strong mouth took on a further twist. 'So maybe
I'd be the one you'd need to watch out for. And the
name is Jake, remember? One more of those
"Professor"'s, and I might be tempted to give you a
foretaste.'

Roger's entry forestalled any reply she might have
made to that threat. They had neither of them been
shouting, so he could have caught little of the actual
words, but there was no mistaking the electric atmosphere. He looked from one to the other of them in obvious perturbance. Jake was the first to break the pause.

'A drink before we eat? Karen, what will you have?'

Suddenly aware of the tremor in her lower limbs, she made a supreme effort to regain her equilibrium. 'Anything but the vodka, please. It *was* a bit too strong.'

There was no acknowledgement of the concession in his brief nod. He took Roger's request for a whisky, and went to fetch the drinks from a cabinet on the far side of the spacious room, leaving the two of them to take a seat side by side on one of the sofas.

'What was all that about?' asked Roger *sotto voce*. 'Or should I guess?'

'I need you to make things clear to him,' Karen acknowledged. 'You wouldn't have brought me along if you didn't need me.'

Something flickered in his eyes. 'True,' he agreed.

'So when *are* you going to tell him?'

'As soon as I get the chance.' He sounded abrupt. 'Just leave it for the moment, will you, Karen? This isn't the time or place.'

So when and where would be the right time or place? she wondered hollowly, feeling doubt start to creep in. If Roger allowed himself to be out-gunned by Jake, where would that leave her? She was hardly going to be paid for sitting around twiddling her thumbs until he got back.

CHAPTER TWO

DINNER was a serve-yourself meal, with a choice from various covered tureens set out on a heated side-table in the small dining salon. The owner didn't, Jake said, retain a big enough staff to offer waiter service. Karen had the feeling he also disapproved of that kind of servility—an attitude with which she could concur. Having the food itself prepared by someone else was bonus enough.

The following day's filming schedule was the main topic of conversation throughout the meal. With her role still uncertain, Karen felt unable to make much of a contribution. She could sense Jake's eyes on her from time to time, but she refused to glance his way. If Roger failed to come through it was going to be up to her to change the man's mind somehow. She was going to need to marshal all her reserves in order to do so.

The meal over, the party moved out on to the wide balcony for brandies and coffee. Karen took her glass and strolled along to the nearest corner on the pretext of examining the colourful vines clinging to the wall. The sky overhead was pinpricked with stars—the same stars looking down on the Mayan ruins deep in the jungles of Petan. Some had been found, a few excavated, many more lost forever under the encroaching growth. The site to which Jake Rothman was hopefully to lead his team had already been discovered some months ago by the Indian guide who was his friend and associate from previous expeditions, but that didn't mean

20

he would be able find it again without difficulty. In this climate, all signs of passage through the forest would be obliterated within days.

She hadn't heard anyone approaching, and was startled when Roger spoke at her elbow.

'Don't look so downcast. It will all be sorted out by this time tomorrow.'

'Why not tonight?' Karen asked. 'If it's going to happen at all then surely it's better sooner rather than later?'

He shook his head. 'Give Jake time to come round to the idea on his own. Let him see how much a part of the team you are. In the meantime, you might try a little diplomacy. Antagonising the man isn't going to help.'

'In other words, you don't have the authority to insist on taking me along?' she countered softly, and received a wry shrug.

'It would hardly be good policy to try laying down the law, considering he's the kingpin of the whole operation. I've no doubts about your capabilities in any sphere, Karen, but he doesn't know you.'

'You've only known me a few months yourself,' she pointed out. 'What makes *you* so sure I can handle things?'

'Your whole character,' he said. 'What you lacked in experience four months ago you more than made up for in sheer will to succeed. Your spare-time activities take care of the fitness aspect. I don't imagine roughing it will faze you one iota.'

'I don't imagine it will either,' Karen acknowledged. 'The problem is in convincing our lord and master over there.' She summoned a brief smile. 'He seems to think I'll prove too much of a strain on general ethics.'

'Maybe it's his own he's doubtful about.' Roger sounded a little short. 'Are you going to rejoin the party, or would you prefer to turn in? You realise it's almost four-thirty in the morning our time?'

Jet lag was probably one of the reasons she was feeling so down, Karen reflected. A good night's sleep would set her right again.

'I think I'll turn in,' she said. 'Tomorrow's likely to be a busy day.'

Jake was facing the pair of them as they came along the balcony. He looked from one to the other of them without change of expression, but there was something in the blue gaze that brought sudden realisation to Karen at least. If he was under the impression that there was something already going on between her and Roger, that could well be the crux of his objections to her inclusion in the party. The sooner she scotched that idea the better.

'We'll none of us be far behind you,' said Mike when she announced her intention of calling it a day. His smile was over-intimate. 'Sweet dreams.'

'We're going to need a reasonably early start in the morning,' claimed Roger. 'No later than nine. I'd hope to be through with the city shots by mid-afternoon. We can have the museum from five till six-thirty.'

And the morning after would see her on that flight north to Petan, thought Karen determinedly as she made her way to her room. Whatever it took!

About to slide between crisp cotton sheets some twenty minutes or so later, she was arrested by the soft knock on the door. She pulled on a lightweight wrap before going to answer it, conscious of the tautening of muscle and sinew when she saw Jake Rothman standing there.

'Sorry about this, but I need some things for the morning,' he said. 'It will only take a couple of minutes.'

Karen stepped back from the doorway. 'Feel free. It's your house.'

'On loan,' he corrected. He moved across to the wardrobes lining one wall, and opened a door to select a pair of trousers and a shirt from the few items hanging there.

Studying the tapering line of his back down to narrow waist and lean hard hips, she heard herself saying huskily, 'Just in case you're under any illusion, there's nothing going on between me and Roger.'

He turned to look at her, hangers dangling from a finger. There was irony in the line of his mouth. 'Just good friends, eh?'

'I work for him,' she rejoined. 'That's as far as it goes.'

'What makes you think I'd be interested whatever?'

Karen felt her face warm. 'I wasn't telling you from a personal angle, just so that you don't get the wrong idea about why I'm here. Roger sees me with a purely professional eye.'

The irony increased. 'I'd doubt that. You're not built for it.'

'Thanks.' Her tone was frigid.

'A simple statement of fact. You may be good at doing whatever it is you do, but don't run away with the notion that how you look had nothing to do with your getting the job. I've seen the way Halsey looks at you—and he was pretty quick to follow you earlier.'

'He's concerned over the way you're reacting, that's all.' Karen steeled herself to make the attempt. 'Jake, I need this job. If I have to go back there isn't going to be one. Can't you at least give me a chance to prove I shan't be a liability?'

There was no perceptible softening of the blue eyes. 'What kind of trial would you suggest?'

'A week on the road? If I hold you up, or back, or cause you any kind of other problem, then I'll pull out.'

'Returning here on your own? How?'

She had given no thought to that aspect because she didn't intend it to happen. Her shrug made light of the omission. 'I'm sure you'd work something out.'

His smile lacked humour. 'There'd be no coming back, and you know it, so the answer is still the same. You'd better get some sleep.'

'It's down to Roger in the end,' she retorted, losing all patience in the face of his intractability. 'He needs me!'

The strong mouth twisted. '"Wants" might be closer.'

'There's nothing of that nature. How many times do I have to say it?' Karen was too incensed to heed Roger's earlier warning. 'If anyone's professionalism is in doubt I'd say it's yours for allowing prejudice to influence your judgement. The women you know might be good for one thing and one thing only, but I'm not one of them!'

A spark lit the blue eyes as he studied her. When he moved it was with purpose, dropping the clothing he held to the floor as he came towards her. Karen stood her ground. She refused to lift even a finger in defence when he pulled her into his arms and bent his head to find her mouth in a kiss that seared.

Only no amount of will-power could cool the swift spread of heat through her veins, nor still the pounding of her heart against her ribcage. She felt her body move involuntarily closer—felt her breasts come into contact with the hardness of his chest. Only then did she start fighting his hold on her, although it did her little good.

She was quivering with mingled chagrin, fury and some other emotion she didn't care to examine too closely when he finally let her go. The sardonic smile playing about his lips served to fan the flames.

'The objection came a mite late for total conviction,' he observed. 'You'd need to practise more. See you in the morning—Karen.'

She stood biting her lip as he left the room. The fact that she had more than half asked for some form of retaliation didn't help. If there had been any chance at all of persuading him to change his attitude before, there was none at all now. Which left everything down to Roger. Not an encouraging thought after what he had said earlier.

Not surprisingly, considering that it was around five o'clock in the morning British time, she was asleep within minutes of her head touching the pillow, awakening to sunlight and a sense of disorientation. Memory brought despondency to join it. In another twenty-four hours, if Jake had his way, she would be waving goodbye to a whole lot more than a jungle trek. Her whole future career could be in jeopardy.

Although it was only just gone six-thirty, she knew she wouldn't sleep again. After showering, she donned khaki trousers and shirt, contenting herself with a touch of lipstick and a comb through her hair before leaving the room.

It was deliciously cool and fresh outside. At five thousand feet above sea-level, Guatemala City enjoyed a spring-like climate all year round. The morning sky was a high clear blue, the only cloud to be seen at present wreathing the higher points of the distant mountains.

Leaning on the stone balustrade, Karen breathed in the scent from the massed flowers below. From what she had read, the Petan jungles were dense with plant life of all kinds, including flowers renowned for their size and beauty. Animal life too, although the chances of encountering a jaguar or puma were supposedly remote. She wanted so badly to go there—to experience the thrill first hand. Why, oh, why did Jake Rothman have to be the fly in the ointment?

'Sleep well?' asked Mike lightly, coming out to join her. 'I had a pretty restless night myself. Can't imagine why.' He cast a sideways glance when she failed to respond. 'Too bad Rothman's proving difficult. The man has his priorities all wrong.'

Karen allowed herself a faint smile and a shrug. 'You could say that.'

'So what are you planning on doing about it?'

'I don't know,' she acknowledged. 'I don't suppose there's a whole lot I *can* do about it.'

'Roger can, though.'

She shook her head. 'When it comes right down to it, the professor is more important to the enterprise than I am.'

Mike laughed. 'Not from where I'm standing!'

Which was too close, she acknowledged drily. She straightened unhurriedly away from the balustrade. 'I can smell coffee.'

The rest of the party was already gathered in the dining salon. Jake nodded to her briefly when she came in, then carried on with what he was saying.

'I ordered the cars to be brought round for eight-thirty. You three with the equipment in one, Howard, the rest of us in the other.'

'We shan't be doing too much city shooting,' put in Roger, as though deciding it was high time he asserted some authority. 'Just the contrasts between old and new. There's none of it exactly ancient anyway, considering it was only founded in 1776, but it's a good starting-point. There are Mayan artefacts on show in the museum. I've also arranged for the plane taking us up north tomorrow to do a fly-over on the city—a kind of farewell to modern civilisation for the next few weeks.'

'Are you still planning to visit Tikal?' asked Karen, determined not to be left out of the discussion at least.

'Too touristy,' declared Jake before the younger man could answer. 'And already well covered by just about every Central American travelogue. Chal Luz may not prove as extensive, but we'll be the first to film it.'

Roger said curiously, 'I didn't realise the place had a name already.'

Jake smiled and shook his head. 'It doesn't. Not officially. I named it myself after the man who came across it—Luz Salvador. From what he tells me, the jungle encroachment is fairly light, so we shouldn't have too much difficulty. Whether it will turn out to be worth an archaeological survey remains to be seen. Our only concern is getting there.'

Nothing, Karen told herself resolutely, feeling the buzz of excitement, was going to keep her from making that journey! If she had to follow under her own steam, she would even do that. How, she wasn't sure. By bus, if all else failed. The fact that any road journey into El Petan was likely to take many hours was something to be considered if and when.

The day got under way with the arrival of the two Land Rovers, driven by cheerful and friendly Hispanics. Jake chose to take the front passenger seat, leaving Karen and Roger to share the rear.

Gazing at the back of the dark head, Karen couldn't help noting the healthy shine of hair untouched by any form of gel or other dressing. The crisp line into the nape of his neck made her fingers suddenly itch to reach out and touch. Last night's kiss had left an indelible imprint on both mind and lip, although the latter had to be more imagination than fact.

Physical attraction took little note of the finer emotions, she acknowledged wryly. Not that last night had been intended as anything but a salutary lesson on Jake's part. She was no more his type than he was hers.

Many of the older buildings of Guatemala Ciudad had been destroyed by earthquakes, those remaining now interspersed with modern high rise structures. Its wide avenues were thronged with motorised traffic. A steel-girded tower, built along the lines of the Eiffel, straddled one of the main thoroughfares.

'Erected in commemoration of Justo Rufino Barrios,' advised Jake in answer to Karen's comment. 'One of the country's national heroes.'

'He's the one who tried to restore unity to Central America, isn't he?' she hazarded with dim recollection of seeing the name mentioned in some book she had read.

'That's right.' There was a note of surprise in his voice. 'You've obviously done some homework.'

'I believe in finding out as much background detail as I can about any project I aim to tackle,' she came back with deliberation. 'I also read up on the Maya civilisation.'

'All knowledge is useful,' he acknowledged drily. 'Even if it's only for completing crossroads.'

With Roger maintaining silence on the subject, she had no choice but to let the moment pass. Only it wasn't going to stop at that, she vowed. One way or another, she was going on that expedition!

First stop was at the lovely twin-towered cathedral. Standing in the park-like square fronting it, Jake made a brief appearance, speaking from a memorised script. He would be writing the general commentary after they got back, when the final editing was completed. Once in Petan, the filming would be on a day-to-day basis, using the fly-on-the-wall technique in part.

For the eventual viewers, Karen reflected, it would be almost like being there, sharing both the triumphs and tribulations of the journey as they occurred. There would be more film shot than would ever be used, of course; it was the editing that set the standard for a production. Badly handled, it could finish up as a series of events with little cohesion instead of an unfolding storyline. There was no chance of that happening with Roger in charge. He was brilliant at his job.

The six of them lingered over a late luncheon in a back-street café recommended by Jake. Karen plumped for the *gallo en chicha*, which turned out to be chicken macerated and cooked in alcohol. Somewhat typically, Mike chose the local equivalent of sweetbreads, while the rest went for various kinds of tortillas. Roger firmly limited the wine consumption for all. The last thing he needed, he declared, was a drunken crew out at the museum.

'We're invited to the local equivalent of a barbecue tonight, by the way,' announced Jake over cups of the thick sweet coffee. 'I took the liberty of accepting for all, considering it's going to be our last opportunity to relax socially for some time.'

'Glad I didn't bother packing my tux,' quipped Mike. 'Sounds a great idea!' His glance shifted to Karen. 'If there's dancing, I claim first privilege.'

'What makes you think I'm included?' she responded levelly, and saw Jake's mouth acquire a twist.

'I'd hardly be leaving you out.'

'Why not?' There was a challenge in her steady gaze. 'I'm not exactly an acknowledged member of the unit.'

Blue eyes returned her gaze without expression. 'Hardly the same thing.'

'It is to me.'

'Your choice.' He appeared totally unmoved. 'You're on Saturday's flight out via Panama City, by the way.' He caught her swift glance in Roger's direction, and shook his head. 'We already discussed it.'

Roger lifted his shoulders in a wry shrug. 'Sorry, Karen, but it makes sense. You'll be OK. I'll see to that.'

'Thanks.' It was all she could find to say. Faced with his withdrawal, Karen knew it came down to a straight choice: she could either follow her somewhat nebulous plan to trail the party under her own steam, or give in and return home to England and a future by no means certain, regardless of what Roger might promise.

A choice she hadn't really expected to have to make, she was bound to admit. Now that it came down to it, the pitfalls involved in the first were becoming all too glaringly obvious. It would take too long by road. They would probably have vanished into the jungle long before she reached the village from where they were to pick up their guide. Finding someone both willing and able to follow them would be by no means a certainty either.

In which case she would simply have to retrace her steps and accept the situation, came the fatalistic thought. At least she would have tried. That had to be better than just sitting back and taking it.

If Jake was surprised by her lack of resistance, he gave no sign. Catching Nigel's eye across the table, Karen felt cheered by the look of genuine regret and sympathy she saw there. As an assistant himself, he obviously felt for her more deeply than the others in the team. Mike's only regret would be purely personal, while Howard probably didn't care one way or the other. As for Roger...

Not exactly his fault, she reasoned, trying to be fair. No matter how brilliant the photography and direction, it was Jake Rothman's name that drew public interest to the subject matter, which gave the man a whole lot of clout. He didn't want her on the team, so she had to be dispensed with.

They reached the museum just after closing time at five to find a one-man staff left to admit them to the premises. Looking around the section devoted to the Mayan culture while waiting for Howard and Nigel to set up the portable lighting, Karen was mesmerised by the artefacts on show. Some of the pottery pieces were intact in every detail, embellished with painted cranes and flying parrots, with men and gods. There were jade vases, bowls and plaques, the cold green wonderfully carved.

'Yum Kaax, the corn god,' said Jake almost at her shoulder as she studied one such piece. 'Handsome young man, wasn't he?'

'Very,' she agreed, controlling her start. 'Did the Mayans go in for human sacrifice to the gods?'

'Some, though the Toltecs and Aztecs were the real bad guys in that line.'

Karen forced a light note. 'Hardly the kind of comment I'd expect from someone in your position.'

'It sums it up well enough,' came the dry response.

'Suited to my supposed intellect, you mean?'

'Only if you want to see it that way.' He had moved up into her line of vision, standing there at her side with hands thrust casually into trouser pockets as he looked into the show-case. 'As a woman of undoubted intelligence, you should be able to appreciate my point of view regarding this project.'

'If it's acceptance and approval you're looking for you came to the wrong place,' she returned shortly. 'You're the only one with doubts as to my ability.'

He gave an impatient sigh. 'You've no idea what conditions are like out there. Jungle travel is no picnic. If the heat and sheer hard slog didn't get to you, the insects certainly would. Apart from the mosquitoes and termites, there are things which burrow under the skin and——'

'Chiggers and ticks,' Karen interrupted. 'I know all that. It didn't put me off before; it doesn't put me off now. In fact, I'd be willing to bet I could take it better than most.'

Jake turned his head to study her with an expression difficult to read in the blue eyes. 'I'm almost tempted——' He broke off at the sound of her name being called, shaking his head. 'Forget it. You'd better go and join your boss.'

She went with reluctance. Given a few minutes longer, she might well have managed to persuade him to change his mind. The fact that he had weakened even momentarily afforded some faint hope. There was still the evening to work on him. All she needed was a convincing line.

CHAPTER THREE

BOTH looking and sounding like a xylophone, the marimba was so long that it needed five players in line to cover all the keys. Karen found the music they produced highly enjoyable, if a little lacking in variety.

'Wouldn't go down too well on *Top of the Pops*,' commented Mike, obviously not over-impressed. 'Still, beggars can't be choosers. How about that dance?'

There were others already on the wooden sub-floor which had been laid over the oval swimming-pool. Lit by tree-strung fairy lights, the grounds of the luxurious villa were awash with people of varied nationalities. Karen had anticipated something a little more low-key than this beautifully organised event. Clad in clean but practical shirt and trousers, she felt at a distinct disadvantage beside the other women, wearing bright and pretty dresses.

Stifling reluctance, she accompanied the sound engineer. He pulled her close when they reached the floor, the hand at her waist beginning an immediate slide downwards.

'Cut it out, Mike,' she said coolly, conscious of possible watching eyes. 'We're here to dance, not wrestle!'

He laughed, not in the least put off. 'You can't blame a man for trying. That *derrière* of yours is an out and out temptation!'

'One you'll just have to resist,' she returned. 'Don't ruin any chance I might still have of coming on this job.'

'I thought that question had already been settled,' he said. 'Not that I agree with the decision. You'd have been an asset in more ways than the one. Can you imagine how dull it's going to be with no female company to lighten our days—to say nothing of the nights?'

Karen chose to ignore the last. Mike might like to act the lecher, but it took two to make anything of it. Given no encouragement, he would eventually lose interest.

'It still isn't too late for a change of mind,' she said. 'There are several hours to go before you leave for Petan.'

'Most of them in bed.' Breath warm on her cheek, he added softly, 'Unless you're planning on seducing the man into taking you along.'

She kept her tone level. 'I doubt very much if Jake Rothman could be swayed that way, even if I were willing to try it. Unlike some not too far away.'

'If you mean me, the problem wouldn't have arisen in the first place. Howard was none too keen on the idea, though, it has to be admitted.'

Too bad, Karen thought. Jake was the one she had to convince. The only encouragement she had to cling to was that momentary hesitation at the museum earlier. If she could talk with him alone again, she might just be able to get through to him. When, was the question.

Right now he was dancing with the woman who was their hostess. Dark and beautiful, the other looked to be of Spanish blood, although her name, Elaine Sleeman, sounded English enough. Though she wore a gold ring on her left-hand third finger, no husband had yet put in an appearance. Widowed, or divorced, perhaps? Whichever, she obviously appealed to Jake, who was looking down at her with an indulgent smile on his lips.

The kind of indulgence she could do with a little of herself, thought Karen sourly. Except that Elaine wasn't trying to knuckle in on any male bastions, was she? Imagining the woman in any kind of setting lacking in civilised refinements was next to impossible. She was pure luxury from the top of her shining head to the tips of her Gucci shoes. The white dress in between might be cotton, but it was certainly not off-the-peg. It fitted her superbly structured figure to perfection.

'Some looker, isn't she?' commented Mike, becoming aware of the other couple. 'Rich too. Husband died last year after less than eighteen months of marriage.'

'How do you know that?' asked Karen.

'I asked around,' he said. 'There's never any shortage of people willing to gossip—especially where it concerns a beautiful woman left a fortune by a man fifty years older.' His laugh was low and suggestive. 'It's to be hoped she made it worth his while!'

'She may even have loved him,' Karen returned drily. 'It's not beyond the realms of possibility.'

'Her type loves number one best, although, from the way she's looking at Rothman right now, he's running pretty close. Seems he knew her before she married this Sleeman chap. You can write your own scenario around that.'

'Are you suggesting there might have been some kind of...arrangement between them?'

'Why not? It's happened before. Beautiful younger woman marries besotted rich old man and drives him into an early grave to inherit his money so that she and lover can enjoy the fruits.'

'That's ridiculous!' Karen was fired by some emotion that went rather deeper than mere scorn. 'Even if Jake did know her first, he's hardly a pauper himself!' She caught the glint of amusement in Mike's eyes and pulled herself up a little sheepishly. 'You have a warped sense of humour!'

'Just mild exaggeration,' he said unrepentantly. 'If it comes to that, how do you know so much about Rothman's finances?'

'I don't,' she confessed. 'I simply——'

'Pure supposition, you mean. Not that I think you're all that wrong, as it happens. I hear he's a shrewd investor.'

'I'm not really interested.' The denial was short. 'Let's take a break.'

Mike shrugged. 'Fine with me. The music's not my bag, anyway.'

The others in their group had gone to get food from the laden trestles. Karen picked up a plate and joined Roger in choosing from the many and varied dishes. The smell of roast pork from one spitted carcass was overpowering.

'Enjoying it?' he asked.

'I might enjoy it better,' she returned with deliberation, 'if I were sure of my job.'

'You still have a job,' he assured her. 'You'll be kept busy until I get back. I don't want to lose you, Karen.'

There was something in the way he said that last which brought sudden doubt. Much as she admired and liked Roger, she wanted no deeper involvement. Reading too much into too little, she reassured herself. He was simply referring to their working relationship.

'There might still be a chance of persuading Jake to take me along if you try again,' she said. 'Who's going to do all the mundane note-taking, timing, et cetera, if I'm not there?'

'Nigel, I suppose. I hadn't really thought about it.' He sounded rueful. 'Jake isn't going to change his mind.

He made the position pretty clear first thing this morning. Either you go or he goes.'

'Could he really withdraw from a contract that way?' she asked. 'In fact, would he really attempt it if it came right down to it?'

'With Jake Rothman there's no knowing what he might do. He's a law unto himself. He's right, anyway. I shouldn't have brought you.'

'Don't you start on that tack too!' she said disgustedly. 'You thought me able enough before all this.'

'Able, yes, but I didn't give enough thought to the other aspects.'

'One woman, five men, you mean?'

He cast her a swift glance. 'Something like that.'

'There's safety in numbers. Different if it were one to one, perhaps.' She paused before adding, '*Will* you try him again, Roger?'

'It's too late,' he said. 'Your flight is already booked.'

'It can always be cancelled.'

He shook his head. 'It would be a waste of time.'

She said stubbornly, 'Then do you have any objection to my raising the subject with him again myself?'

'For what good it will do, go right ahead. I'll be no worse off.' He gave her a wry smile. 'The islands series we're scheduled to do next shouldn't present any problems.'

It presented little interest at present either, Karen was bound to acknowledge, although it would take them far afield. She had to prove herself here first.

Round tables were set at intervals about the roped-off eating section. Jake had joined Howard at one of them, although not apparently interested in food. Karen took the chair next to him because it happened to be the first one she came to, and it would have looked too pointed to pass it by, placing her plate down on the table without over-much interest in the food it contained.

He must have left the delectable Mrs Sleeman shortly after she and Mike had vacated the dance-floor, she thought, toying with a chicken drumstick. She was vitally aware of the muscular thigh almost brushing her own, of the tanned forearm resting on the cloth, long, clever fingers toying idly with a wine glass.

In profile, his face looked chiselled from stone, saved from total austerity only by the sensual curve of his lower lip. The memory of those same lips on hers sent a tremor right through her. The man had charisma; there was no doubting that. Liking or disliking had nothing to do with the way he affected her.

The same way, judging from appearances, that he affected Elaine Sleeman. For a moment she found herself wondering if there could possibly be any truth in Mike's hypothesis, before dismissing the idea out of hand. It was all too preposterous—the kind of thing that only happened in hackneyed novels or films. If there was something going on between them now, they were both of them free agents.

'Not hungry?' asked the subject of her thoughts, making her start because she had believed him totally immersed in conversation. 'You've done everything with that drumstick except eat it!'

'Not quite everything,' she retorted, making a fast recovery. 'They make a nice nose ornament, I'm told.'

'Only if you have one big enough to take it, and you hardly qualify on that score.' He brought up a hand to run a light finger down the short straight length in emphasis, mouth slanting at her involuntary jerk away. 'If you're not going to eat, maybe you'd like to dance again instead?'

About to refuse, Karen caught herself up. Wasn't this the very chance she had been looking for? Avoiding Roger's eye, she gave a smiling shrug and got to her feet. 'Why not?' she asked lightly. 'It might give me an appetite.'

There were only two other couples on the floor at present. A little taller than average for a woman herself, Karen found that her eyes still only came level with the base of Jake's throat when he held her. His grasp was light, yet she was conscious of each and every fingerprint at her centre back. Unlike Mike, he kept the hand in one place.

'I gather this isn't exactly your kind of event,' he said.

'It isn't quite what I expected,' she prevaricated. 'How did you come to meet Mrs Sleeman—Elaine?'

'Elena,' he corrected. 'You must have misheard. I've known her family for several years. I was at university with her elder brother. The first time I came out to Guatemala I was invited to stay with the Domingos.'

'I see.' Karen waited a brief moment before adding, 'Did you know her husband too?'

'Not to any extent. He was something of a recluse.' Jake's voice had become brusque. 'If you've been listening to the gossips you'd better get the story right. Elena married Sleeman to save her father from bankruptcy. Anything she's gained from the sacrifice she merits.'

'I wasn't prejudging,' Karen began, then stopped, ashamed of the lie. 'Well, yes, I suppose I was. I'm sorry.'

'I'm not the one owed an apology. Not that Elena would want it either. She prefers to turn a deaf ear to the talk.' The brusqueness was still there. 'Shall we change the topic?'

A good time or not, Karen seized on the opening. 'Willingly. What were you going to say this afternoon when Roger called me?'

He made no attempt to feign ignorance. 'A temporary weakness. I haven't changed my mind. There's no place for you.'

The tightness in her throat roughened her voice. 'So much the man in charge, aren't you? You'd even use blackmail to get your own way!'

The hand at her back tautened, bringing her in closer. 'Blackmail?'

'Isn't that what you told Roger—that either I go or you do?' She was aware with every fibre of the hard lean length of him; of the power to crush in the arms enfolding her. 'I'd have thought the project rather more important to you than that.'

'The project,' he said, 'is *too* important to risk having it disrupted by any sexual element. If you were in your fifties, and ugly with it, it might be different.'

'If I were in my fifties I probably wouldn't be fit enough to make it, anyway,' Karen responded smartly. 'A couple of days in the kind of conditions you're talking about and sex will be the last thing anyone is going to be thinking about!'

There was irony in the reply. 'Sure it will. For the last time, the answer is no! Now, be a good girl and accept it.'

That did it, she thought savagely. She was going on that expedition if it killed her! The village where they were to meet Luz was some couple of hours by road from San Samoza, where the plane was to drop them, and she had already ascertained from the guide book she had brought with her that a daily bus service, calling at San Samoza among other places, left for Flores in

Petan mid-morning. It was going to be approaching midnight before she eventually reached her destination, but she wouldn't allow that to put her off. Nothing was going to put her off now.

'You win,' she said on a note of resignation. 'I'm through arguing.'

'Good.' The arms holding her relaxed again. 'You're hard to convince.' There was a pause before he tagged on unexpectedly, 'Tell me about yourself. What made you choose this business in the first place?'

'We did a sixth-form project on various career paths,' she acknowledged, surprised by the request. 'Television production appealed to me then.'

'But you didn't go straight into it?'

'No, I took a degree course in history with a view to teaching.'

'Parental urging?'

Karen looked up into shrewd blue eyes, heart registering the impact with a double beat. 'To a certain extent, I suppose. They didn't see a steady future in television.'

'What future do you see for yourself?'

'I want to be where Roger is now,' she came back promptly. 'Not that I'd be liable to get very far if everyone followed your inclinations.'

'I thought we were through with that argument?' His tone had shortened again. 'You're like a dog with a bone!'

There was no point, Karen admitted, in ruining what was left of the evening. By this time tomorrow she should be close to fulfilling her aim. Once there, even Jake had to appreciate her determination. For certain, she wasn't coming back!

'Sorry,' she said in mock penitence. 'Call it a last-gasp stand.'

Whatever reply he might have made to that was lost as one of the servants appeared at his elbow. The man spoke in Spanish, eliciting a sudden frown on Jake's part.

'My turn to be sorry,' he said. 'Something came up. We'll all be leaving shortly, anyway. Early start tomorrow.'

He escorted Karen back to the table where Roger and Howard were still seated, before following the man-servant who had come to fetch him. Watching him thread his way through the milling throng of merrymakers, head and shoulders above the majority, she wondered if it was Elena who had issued the summons—and, if so, why? Jealousy, perhaps, because she had seen him dancing with another woman?

'Made your peace?' asked Roger. 'The two of you looked to be getting along OK out there.'

'Looks can be deceptive,' Karen answered lightly, thinking of Jake's likely reaction to her appearance tomorrow night. It was going to be a shock for Roger too, but she couldn't risk telling him what she had planned in case he flatly forbade it. The job called for total commitment, he had told her at the start. He could hardly take her to task for applying that very quality.

The party was still going strong when they left at midnight. Elena came to see them off. She rested possessive fingers on Jake's arm as she made her farewells.

The two of them had been out of circulation since the summons more than an hour before. Making love, Karen suspected, observing the tell-tale brightness in Elena's dark eyes, the general air of satisfaction in her demeanour. It was difficult to read anything from Jake's expression.

'You must all of you visit with me on your return from Petan,' declared the Spanish woman in heavily accented

English. Her gaze rested fleetingly and dismissively on Karen. 'Such a pity that you had a wasted journey, but there are places where no woman should venture.'

'Oh, I'm sure you're right,' Karen returned, tongue-in-cheek. 'Thank you for your hospitality, anyway.'

The dark head inclined. 'You are welcome.'

Jake lingered to say a final word of goodbye in private before coming to slide into the waiting taxi. Seated with Roger in the back, Karen closed her eyes and pretended to doze as they threaded through the streets. Both men were silent too, each apparently preoccupied with his own thoughts. Roger would be thinking about the job ahead. Of that she was fairly certain. Jake might well have other matters on his mind at present. Twenty-four hours from now, Karen could expect to be the subject under review, but she refused to allow *that* thought to deter her. Actions spoke louder than words.

There was a general and immediate move towards retirement on reaching the house. The main party was due to leave for the airport at eight o'clock.

'I'll be up and about to see you all off,' promised Karen smoothly when wished a good journey of her own by Nigel. 'I don't intend wasting my day mooching around.'

'Just watch out for pickpockets if you decide to do any shopping,' warned Jake. 'Especially round the central market area. They're on the look-out for tourists.' His gaze lingered for a brief moment on her face, his mouth taking on a faint sardonicism. 'See you later.'

Safe in her room, Karen took the time to reorganise her scanty baggage. The real organisation would take place at Fuentas Santos, where Luz would have gathered supplies for the trek. With the first part of the journey to be made by boat, life should be relatively simple. Only when they took to the jungle itself would weight become a matter for concern. No doubt there would be extra help available to spread the load, but she would naturally expect to carry her share.

Jake must have been in at some time to see to his own things. The framed backpack standing ready in a corner looked well used and totally professional. Roughing it was no novelty for him. He had travelled over much of South and Central America in his time. Last year he had traced the Inca road from Cuzco through to Bogotá— a journey of more than three thousand miles. Karen had been enthralled by his account of the journey in one of the geographical magazines. It was that, as much as anything else, which made her so determined to experience it all for herself. Different, indeed, from the kind of country she was accustomed to trekking through, but all the more enticing for it.

With her mind full of the coming day's challenge, she found sleep difficult to come by. Eventually she gave up and went to find a drink to ease the dryness in her throat.

The kitchen lay beyond the dining-room. Modern and functional, it boasted a huge refrigerator in addition to numerous cupboards. Finding a glass in one of the latter, Karen poured herself a generous measure of the freshly squeezed orange juice left ready for morning, and took it out on to the balcony.

The night air was deliciously cool and fragrant: too cool to stay out in for long wearing nothing but thin cotton pyjamas, but five minutes wasn't going to hurt. That the climate in Petan would be very different from this, she was well aware. Heat and humidity would be the order of the day—and night too. One of the crosses to be borne. She had come prepared to take anything the job might throw at her.

'You should have something on your feet,' said Jake from the doorway behind her. 'You never know what you might step on.'

Karen had stiffened involuntarily on the first syllable; she forced herself to speak calmly and levelly. 'You have a nasty habit of creeping up on people.'

'There's no monopoly on sleeplessness.' He was moving as he spoke, coming forward to lean his elbows on the balustrade at her side. 'Nor on fresh air.'

He was wearing a pair of shorts and nothing else. Karen was acutely conscious of the dark whorls of body hair on his bare chest—could feel her nipples come suddenly and tinglingly erect.

'A concession to circumstances,' he advised, sensing her glance. 'I prefer to sleep nude.'

'Saves on the washing, I suppose,' she retorted. 'Are you always nervous before a new venture?'

'There are more reasons for sleeplessness than nervousness.' He sounded more amused than affronted. 'Frustration, for one.'

The reply was out before she could stop it. 'Not something I'd imagine *you're* suffering from tonight!'

He turned his head to study her, one dark brow lifted. 'Tell me more.'

'I meant,' she said hastily, 'that if anyone is frustrated it's me.'

'No, you didn't.' His tone was almost conversational. 'You were talking about Elena. Leaving aside the fact that it's damn-all to do with you or anyone else, what makes you so sure you're right?'

Her shrug was meant to be casual. 'Most women are capable of reading the signs.'

'In my experience, most women see only what they want to see. Why the interest, anyway?'

'I am not,' she stated grimly, 'interested in *any* of your affairs!'

'Not the impression you've been giving tonight. Not,' he tagged on, 'that I have time to conduct all that many, anyway. However, any advice I can give, feel free to ask.'

She said it between her teeth. 'You'd be the last person I'd ask *anything* of!'

'You're magnificent when you're angry—did you know that?' His voice was mocking. 'A regular green-eyed virago! Roger's a brave man to take you on.'

'I told you, there's nothing between us!'

The mockery increased. 'I meant as an assistant.'

'No, you didn't! You——' She broke off, biting her lip, that slow smile of his a goad to the anger churning inside her. 'I'd have thought you above petty retaliation,' she tagged on with force.

Blue eyes narrowed to twin points as he surveyed her taut features. 'If you thought that petty,' he said softly, 'you might prefer this...'

Last night's kiss had been meant as a chastisement more than anything else, but this time was different. Drawn up close against the lean, hard, near-naked body, feeling his lips pressuring hers apart, she lost all will to fight. His hands felt warm through the thin cotton, burning into her back as he slid them down to find the bottom of her jacket—warmer still on her bare skin. Long tensile fingers traced out her ribcage, drawing a muffled gasp from her throat as they found her breast.

Touch feather-light, he circled the aureole with a fingertip, making her quiver like a leaf inside. She wanted to seize his wrist and pull him to her, to feel the strong, firm hand totally enclose her tingling, aching flesh. She kissed him back feverishly, wantonly, not thinking of anything beyond this moment.

'Let's go inside,' he murmured against her lips.

Head floating, she allowed him to turn her, to guide her back indoors. The arm about her shoulders felt so wonderfully possessive. She could hear the thud of his heart on a level with her ear, and was aware of her own going like a trip hammer. Somewhere at the back of her mind was the knowledge that she was going to regret this, only her body was paying no heed. Her blood sang in her veins.

It took the sight of the bed in her room to start bringing her back to her senses. If she allowed Jake to make love to her on the strength of a basic physical attraction she would be forfeiting every ounce of self-respect she still possessed. Much as she wanted it, she had to find the strength of mind to say no—and mean it.

'You left it a little late for token gestures,' Jake said softly when she attempted to pull away. 'I don't play that kind of game.'

'I made a mistake,' she came back desperately as he began unfastening the buttons of her pyjama top. She clutched at his hands, attempting to prise his fingers away. 'Don't, Jake! I don't want this!'

His lips twisted. 'You're a liar,' he said. 'And a cheap one, at that. What's the next line? Take me with you and I'll come through?'

Anger swept away the last remaining vestige of uncertainty. Eyes flaring, she brought up a hand in an open-palmed slap across one tanned cheek, rocking his head to one side with the force of it. For a fleeting moment he seemed to freeze; she saw the imprint of her fingers on the taut brown skin, the jerk of muscle along his jawline as his teeth clamped together. Then he was turning back to look at her, blue eyes narrowed to icy points of light.

'Not only a dated reaction,' he said, 'but one that begs reprisal. I'll give you a choice.'

Any regret Karen might have felt was swamped by the fresh surge of anger. 'So, hit me back!' she invited, and offered her cheek.

The smile touching his lips had nothing to do with humour. 'If I did, it wouldn't be your face I'd slap, believe me! Anyway, I changed my mind. I prefer retaliation in kind.'

They were back to square one, came the thought as he tautened the grip he still had on her jacket front to pull her up to him. Except that there was nothing even remotely lover-like in the harsh, demanding pressure of his lips on hers now.

Bringing his free arm round behind her waist, he swung her off her feet and carried her over to the bed. Karen made an attempt to roll away from him, but he was too quick for her, pinioning her with his weight as he found her mouth again with that same hard fury. She was aware of his arousal—aware too of the answering fire deep inside her. Despite everything, she wanted this man.

So why, asked another part of her mind, was she fighting him? Why not allow matters to take their course? He would gentle if she responded. *Making* her respond was what he was after.

There was no choice, anyway, because her body was already giving up on the struggle, softening under him, moulding to him, her lips beginning to answer, arms stealing over the wide bare shoulders, fingers seeking the ripple of muscle beneath the smooth skin.

Her pyjama jacket had come open all the way. Jake lifted himself on an elbow to study her, though making no attempt to touch her.

'Nice,' he said. 'A pleasure, however, I'm about to forgo.' He levered himself upright with a forceful movement to sit on the mattress edge, looking down at her with hard mockery. 'Cover yourself, before you catch a chill.'

Fingers numb, Karen pulled both edges of the garment together. She was only just beginning to appreciate his purpose—if 'appreciate' was the right word. She said huskily, 'So very strong-minded of you!'

'Isn't it, though?' There was irony in his smile. 'One of the hardest sacrifices I ever made, but worthwhile if it teaches you a well-deserved lesson.'

'What lesson am I supposed to have learned?' she asked.

'To define frustration in context, if you like.' He added cynically, 'You'd be seeing a lot of it if you were coming on this trip. From two members of the party, for sure. All right, so maybe there isn't anything going on between you and Roger at present, any more than there is with Mike, but both of them fancy their chances. The way you just responded, I could hardly trust you to steer clear.'

'That was only...' she began, then broke off, biting her lip over what she had almost revealed.

'Only what?' Jake prompted. 'Sexual desire? I'm well aware that women are as capable as men of wanting sex for sex's sake, but that doesn't mean I'm willing to see that element introduced into any venture I'm a part of.'

'You mean that's your real reason for not taking me along?' Karen demanded, ignoring the imputation for the moment.

He shrugged. 'Main reason, anyway. As I said before, if you were older and ugly it wouldn't be so much of a problem.' He got to his feet, expression suddenly wry. 'I need a cold shower. One aspect where women score.'

Only outwardly, she thought, feeling the quivering need deep down inside. Jake had woken a part of her hitherto barely touched. Not that she was about to tell him that. Let him believe what he wanted to believe. While she detested him the way she did, his opinion of her meant nothing!

This wasn't going to stop her, she vowed as the door closed on him. If anything, tonight's episode had served to strengthen her resolve. It would be worth a lot to see his face when she turned up tomorrow.

CHAPTER FOUR

SAN SAMOZA appeared much like other small towns through which they had passed on that interminable ride. Alighting from the bus on to the darkened dusty street, and watching it pull away again, Karen felt she had well and truly burned her boats. All that remained was to find some means of transportation out to Fuentas Santos.

Easier said than done, perhaps, considering her few words of Spanish, but faint heart never got anywhere. After ten hours on that bus, she could face anything—even muleback if necessary.

Not that it should be. There were cars on the road, and where there was motorised transport there almost certainly had to be a garage. If they couldn't provide transport themselves they could no doubt tell her where else to go.

She chose not to consider the possibility that said garage might well have closed down for the night by now. There was no point in crossing bridges until she came to them.

The others would have reached Fuentas hours ago, of course. They were to spend the night in the solitary hotel before taking to the river under Luz's guidance. All men together, she thought cynically. Well, they were in for a shock—Jake Rothman in particular. Judging from his attitude this morning, he had believed her well and truly put in her place.

It hadn't been anything he had said, just the expression in his eyes on the odd occasion when their glances had happened to clash across the breakfast table. The knowledge that he had seen her half naked, coupled with the memory of his hands on her body, brought a tingling heat to her cheeks even now. She had wanted to reach out and rake her nails down that lean, arrogant face of his—to wipe the unseen smile from his lips. Well, she would be doing just that, if in kind, in another hour or so.

She had felt very bad about deceiving Roger, though. There had been a moment when he'd been saying goodbye that she had been sorely tempted to tell him her plans. He would have to show righteous disapproval of her action, naturally, but she was counting on his private support. The job was all; he could scarcely deny telling her that. Even family had to take a back seat.

What her mother would think of this venture was only too clear. She hadn't wanted her only daughter to move to London at all, much less to a job scheduled to take over her life. With two brothers still living at home, Karen had hardened her heart against emotional commitment, and taken comfort from her father's ungrudging support. Make the most of life, he had said. It only comes once.

The curious look directed her way by a man passing by roused her to action. Smiling, she said haltingly, *'Próximo garaje, por favor?'*

Badly constructed though the phrase might have been, he obviously understood her request. Karen did her best to follow the directions he gave, but was fighting a losing battle until the man hailed another on the far side of the street, who turned out to be able to speak a little English.

The garage would have closed at nine o'clock, he told her, but he was willing to drive her to Fuentas himself for a satisfactory disbursement. The journey would take an hour, but, as he also had to return, the fee would be doubled, of course.

Karen agreed on the sum asked without haggling. Beggars couldn't be choosers. If it occurred to her that accepting a ride from a stranger was a dangerous practice to start with she turned a deaf ear. This seemed to be her only way of getting to Fuentas, so this was the way she had to go.

The vehicle in which she would be making the journey was parked a couple of streets away. Viewing it, Karen had grave doubts that it would make more than half a mile. The bodywork was practically eaten away by rust, the bonnet tied down with string, the tyres, from what she could see of them in the dim street-lighting, near bald.

Inside was scarcely any better. From the feathers festooning the seats, Karen could only guess that the car was normally used to transport stock to market. The dust which arose when she sat down made her sneeze.

Her driver, whose name, it appeared, was Pedro, seemed unperturbed by the ominous rattle when he started the engine. Jolted unmercifully as they traversed the length of the rutted street, Karen clung to her grip and wryly accepted that the coming hour was going to test her stamina in more ways than the one. The smell of petrol, mingled with the aroma from a multitude of hen droppings, made her stomach heave. After this, the jungle would be a rest cure!

Dark and impenetrable, the latter closed about them soon after leaving the town precincts. Moonlight created an eerie atmosphere in which it was easy to imagine hordes of strange and savage beasts lurking behind the encroaching trees. The road was narrow, the surface

pitted with holes, which Pedro made no attempt to avoid.
Probably because there were too many of them *to* avoid,
Karen reckoned. If the car broke down out here they
were going to be in dire straits. She dared not allow
herself to dwell on the possibility.

Pedro's estimate of an hour to Fuentas proved slightly
optimistic. It was coming up to eleven-thirty by the time
they reached the outskirts of the little Guatemalan town.
Less than a quarter of the size of San Samoza, its popu-
lation appeared to have retired for the night. Early to
bed and early to rise seemed to be the general order of
the day out here.

Hardly more prepossessing than the car in which they
had travelled, the ramshackle hotel overlooked the slow-
rolling river. At least there were lights still showing
behind uncurtained windows, and movement to be seen.

Grateful for his lack of curiosity regarding her presence
in this God-forsaken part of the world, Karen added a
substantial tip to the amount agreed with her driver, and
watched the car disappear in the direction it had come
with a sudden sinking feeling in the pit of her stomach.
No turning back now. The music had to be faced.

A wide if somewhat dilapidated veranda fronted the
hotel. Karen took a deep and steadying breath before
pushing through one half of the double swing doors.
She found herself in a room which apparently did double
duty as reception area and bar. A few rough deal tables
were scattered around.

Only one of these was occupied at present. Seated
facing the door, Roger was the first to see her. He looked
turned to stone. Conversation among the group died as
others followed his gaze.

Jake had his back to her. When he turned it was slowly,
face registering little in the way of shock. Almost, Karen

thought fleetingly, as if he had more than half anticipated such a move on her part.

'Surprise, surprise!' she exclaimed, parodying a certain
TV personality. 'Isn't anyone going to offer me a drink?'

'How did you manage it?' asked Mike. He was
grinning, his approval plain for all to see.

'Bus and car,' she said succinctly. She shook her head
as Jake made a move to rise. 'Too late. It's already left.'

'There are others,' he said grimly. 'First thing in the
morning you'll be on your way back to San Samoza.'

Roger made a sudden and decisive gesture. 'Sorry,
Jake, but I can't go along with that. Leaving her in the
city was one thing, out here another. We don't have any
choice but to take her along now, like it or not.' He got
to his feet to rake forward another chair from one of
the empty tables, the smile he directed Karen's way only
faintly reproving. 'You must be shattered. Come and sit
down. Miguel——' with a wave of a hand at the man
hovering behind the desk '—a drink for the lady.' He
looked enquiringly back at Karen as she slid into the
seat he had procured for her. 'I don't think he has any
vodka.'

'I'll settle for a beer, like the rest of you,' she said
with deliberation. 'When in Rome...' Green eyes met
blue across the width of the table. 'I don't accept defeat
easily.'

'Apparently not.' Jake's tone was neutral now, his face
devoid of expression. 'I, on the other hand, know when
I'm beaten. Meet our guide. Luz, this is Karen Lewis,
Roger's assistant. It seems she'll be accompanying us in
the morning.'

The man seated at his side inclined his head politely
in Karen's direction, although, from the look in the dark
eyes, he was no more enamoured of the prospect than

Jake himself. Skin coffee-brown, nose arched above prominent cheekbones, hair straight and black, he revealed a distinct Mayan ancestry. There was certainly nothing servile in his manner.

'You'll be carrying your own pack,' Jake advised Karen, still in the same neutral tones.

'I'd expect to,' she returned, scarcely able to believe that she had won. 'I'll pull my weight, never fear.'

'Not all that much of it to pull,' chimed in Mike. 'Well stacked, though, I'll grant you!'

Karen could have kicked him. The last thing she needed was that kind of talk! Surprisingly, it was Howard who came to her aid.

'Cut it out, Mike,' he said shortly. 'And *leave* it out, will you?'

'Sure.' The sound engineer was unperturbed. 'Stating the obvious, anyway.'

A glass brimming over with a flat brown liquid was placed in front of Karen by the swarthy little man who she assumed was both hotel owner and bartender. She took a cautious sip, resisting the urge to grimace at the bitter taste. She was no beer-drinker normally, so certainly no connoisseur when it came to judging quality.

'Hungry?' asked Roger.

'Not unduly,' she denied, aware of the lateness of the hour and the unlikelihood of food being readily available. 'I took the precaution of buying in some supplies before I boarded the bus.'

'It must have been a long rough journey,' said Nigel, speaking for the first time since her arrival. His admiration was right there in his eyes. 'The terrain we flew over was hardly what you'd call developed.'

Karen smiled at him, seeing the faint flush mount under his skin with a certain resignation. 'I've known worse.' It was a downright lie, but, with Jake listening in, she had no intention of admitting to the rigours of the journey just completed. 'Some of the scenery was pretty spectacular.' She took another swallow from her glass, determined to give the stuff a fair trial. Not that the taste had improved at all. 'What time do we make a start?'

'First light,' said Jake. 'We'll be sleeping early, rising early all the way through. This is the last alcohol we'll any of us be touching until we get back, so make the most of it.'

A commodity she wouldn't miss one iota herself, Karen reflected. Thinking of the morning brought an anticipatory thrill. Approved or unapproved, she was part and parcel of this venture now. Under no circumstances was she going to give Jake cause for complaint.

'We start using mosquito nets as of tonight,' he continued. 'As you might have noticed already, the insect life is pretty rife. Luz, can you rustle up the necessary equipment for Miss Lewis?'

'The name is Karen,' she told the Guatemalan with deliberation. 'Sorry to be such a nuisance.'

'It's no problem,' he returned in excellent English. 'I was asked to prepare for six people in the first place.' He paused before adding, 'You're going to find the facilities here very primitive by your standards.'

'No more than anyone else.' She was determined not to be allocated any special position. 'I've lived without bathrooms before.'

There was no relenting in the steady regard. 'If you'll forgive my saying so, you don't appear as a woman accustomed to making do.'

'Appearances can be deceptive,' she responded. 'I'll be taking along a tube of moisturiser, that's all. The rest I'll leave to nature.'

'Back to basics, eh?' observed Mike irrepressibly. 'One of the few who could get away with it!'

Karen ignored the interjection. Mike's opinion was of no interest to her. Jake's mouth had a slant to it. He didn't believe her capable of leaving behind the trappings of feminine vanity either. Well, she would prove it in the morning when she turned up with skin and mouth unadorned. It would be far less trouble, anyway.

Luz left to obtain the required items from wherever. His own glass still more than half full, Jake pushed back his chair and got up.

'We'll be sleeping out on the rear veranda, by the way. You can either join us, or use one of the rooms.'

It would be cooler out there than in here, Karen reflected, though the insect life would be more profuse. The mosquito nets, however, would take care of that aspect. What Jake was anticipating, she guessed, was her refusal to join the men. Considering that she would be spending the next couple of weeks doing just that, she may as well start right now.

'I'll take the veranda,' she said. 'I assume we'll be using tents after tonight.'

Jake smiled drily. 'There isn't a tent made that will keep out invaders. All they *do* do is keep in the heat. Still interested?'

'I am not,' she came back steadily, 'about to pull out for lack of a tent!'

The dark head inclined. 'There's a toilet out through the back. I'd suggest you use it now and leave it free for the rest of us.'

'Fine.' Not for anything, Karen thought, was she going to allow him to embarrass her. She added with purpose, 'Supposing you show me where.'

'By all means.' He shook his head when she made to pick up the grip she had dropped on the floor at the side of her chair. 'You can sort that out when Luz gets back with your pack. You'll be limited to what you can carry, and that has to include the essential as well as the personal items.'

A dingy corridor led off from the rear of the lobby. It was too narrow to walk two abreast in comfort, so Jake dropped back a pace. Feeling his hand come down hard on her shoulder the moment they were out of sight and sound of the others was no surprise; her suggestion that he show her where the utilities were had been made with the idea of getting the confrontation over and done with early on. She turned at his urging to find herself backed up against the wall as he closed the gap between them.

'You just don't know how to take no for an answer, do you?' he gritted.

'Not from you,' she retorted. 'When I took this job it was on the understanding that I followed wherever I was called on to follow. I'd hardly be worthy of the trust Roger placed in me if I allowed the first little set-back to put me off.'

Blue eyes registered the dig with a dangerous spark. 'He agreed with me in the end.'

'Only because you were holding a gun to his head.' She was past caring what she said, driven only by the need to drive as many barbs as possible into that hide of his. 'Not that I believe you'd really have pulled out if he'd told you to go to hell. Without the TV exposure, you'd fade into relative obscurity.'

'Relative to what?' he asked, then shook his head as if to negate the question. 'Believe what you like. I'm concerned only with the here and now.' The hand still fastened on her shoulder tightened its grip, fingers digging painfully into the bone. 'You're trouble, Karen. Trouble of the kind we could all have done without. You'd better watch yourself every step of the way!'

'Without eyes on stalks I might find that difficult,' she returned cuttingly. 'If there's trouble at all you can rest assured it won't be at my instigation.'

'It doesn't need to be, you little fool! You've even got Nigel foaming at the mouth.'

Her tone was derisive. 'You're given to exaggeration.'

'Am I?' He took her chin in his other hand, forcing her to look directly at him. 'I know what kind of enticement you're capable of putting out. Mike's already aware of it. So is Roger. How do you imagine a few days of living in close confines is going to affect that situation? You'll have them at each other's throats!'

He was hurting her, but she wouldn't show it. He was also far too close, but she wouldn't allow that to govern her either. 'As I said before,' she rejoined with deliberation, 'there are men and men. Why assume you're the only one capable of controlling his urges?'

His smile was mirthless. 'If we're talking about last night, I found it far from easy.'

'Then perhaps it's really yourself you're worried about.' Karen found a brief second to wonder at her own temerity in taunting him this way, but the satisfaction obtained from it outweighed any disquiet. She brought up a hand and used the tip of a finger to lightly trace the line of his lips, aware of the quivering reaction in the pit of her own stomach as she did so. 'Professor

Rothman—scientist extraordinary—to have such human failings!'

The lean body was tensed, his features set in lines that boded ill. When he spoke it was in low but far from soft tones. 'I'm going to take a great deal of pleasure in putting you where you belong.'

Karen widened her eyes at him provocatively, sure of her safety with the others well within yelling distance. 'It takes two, Professor. I doubt if your reputation would be enhanced by any suggestion of rape in the backwoods.'

'Who,' he asked, 'said anything about rape? You were ready enough to go along last night.'

The flush started deep; she was thankful of the dim lighting to conceal it from him. 'A combination of too much wine and not enough sleep,' she claimed. 'You wouldn't find me as receptive again.'

'No?' He lowered his gaze to her mouth, his lips stretching in a slow and meaningful smile as she involuntarily tensed. 'Well, maybe you're right. Anyway, now's not the time to put it to the test. The room you're looking for is two doors along. A bit lacking in refinement, I'm afraid, but I'm sure you'll survive the culture shock.' He let go of her, standing back to give her room. 'Come on back to the lobby when you're through. Luz should be back by then.'

Karen forced herself to move in the direction indicated, to open the said door and enter into the cramped space behind it. Her exclamation of disgust was swiftly cut off before it could penetrate to the ears she was sure were pricked for it. 'Lacking in refinement' was hardly sufficient to describe what amounted to little more than a hole in the concrete floor.

There would be no refinements whatsoever in the jungle, she knew, but it would be infinitely better than this. Calling this place a hotel was the biggest misnomer she had ever come across.

She found her way back to the lobby without difficulty, taking care to keep her face totally expressionless as she met Jake's sardonic glance. Luz had returned. He handed over a sizeable backpack along with a lightweight bed-roll and muslin net. The collection of short aluminium tubes held together with a couple of straps puzzled her. If they weren't taking tents, why these?

'They clip together to form a framework to support your net,' Jake supplied, watching her expression. 'It won't keep everything out, but it will help. If there are no more questions,' he added, 'I'd advise you to sort out your stuff here and now. Time is going to be limited in the morning.'

With no offer of privacy forthcoming, Karen had no choice but to do her repacking in front of them all. Scanty as her wardrobe appeared, some of it would have to be left here to be picked up on return, she realised almost at once. At least there was no shortage of water in the terrain through which they would be travelling. Clothing could be washed through and drip-dried overnight.

Finished at last, she fastened the pack straps and got to her feet. Jake drained his glass and rose with her.

'I'll show you once how to fix your net,' he said. 'After this you'll be expected to do it yourself.'

Karen kept her tone purposely light. 'I dare say I can manage that.'

'I'll come with you,' said Roger. 'This frame contraption is new to me too.'

If it was cooler outside, the difference was only marginal. Better, anyway, than being cooped up in a room probably infested with fleas, among other things, Karen reflected. Small wonder that there appeared to be no other guests here. A wonder, in fact, if anyone ever stayed here by choice. She slapped automatically at the tickle on the side of her neck, resigning herself to the inevitable bites. They would all be suffering from those— Jake and Luz included. Mosquitoes were totally unselective in their attack.

Unlike the front veranda, this section at least looked and felt fairly solid. Watching Jake slot the tubes together to form the light frame over which her net would be suspended, Karen could only admire his economy of movement. That he had done this many times before was only too apparent. Interspersed with periods of lecturing, much of his life was spent under similar conditions. Hardly surprising that he had never married. What woman would be prepared to put up with the constant absences, sometimes for months at a time?

Certainly not Elena Sleeman. Not unless Karen had totally misjudged the lovely Guatemalan. Her kind would demand constant attention. From most men she would get it, too. Jake might be prepared to dance attendance on occasion, but his work came first without a doubt.

'I said, did you get that?' he repeated, jerking her out of her reverie. Voice clipped, he added, 'Were you paying any attention at all, in fact?'

'I got it,' she said.

'Right.' He pulled the frame apart, jumbling up the sections. 'So supposing you show me.'

Roger was already busy putting instruction into practice next door. Dropping to her knees, Karen slotted the pieces together again, propped the result into place and raised a pair of bland green eyes.

'Will that do?'

His lips twitched. 'A regular Girl Guide! Had you thought about what you're going to wear to sleep in? The majority of us will be stripping down to underwear. I'd as soon you stayed relatively well covered. We've little enough sleep coming tonight as it is.'

'I'll manage,' she declared. 'I'd hate to put temptation *anyone's* way!'

'Keep thinking like that,' he advised, ignoring the satire. 'If you're all fixed I'll go see to my own gear.'

He paused to check Roger's efforts on the way, and nodded approval. Karen tore her gaze from the tall, arrogant figure as he moved away, to meet Roger's eyes with a semi-apologetic little shrug.

'Thanks for sticking by me.'

He smiled. 'Considering the trouble you went to to get here, I couldn't have done anything else. You're one in a million, Karen!'

'All part of the job,' she came back lightly. 'Where my lord and master goeth, there go I!'

'You'll be in for a rise when we get back,' he promised. 'I don't intend letting you get away from me.'

Karen chose not to heed any possible ambiguity in that statement. She had enough on her plate to be going on with.

CHAPTER FIVE

STRUNG out along the length of the veranda, the seven netted mounds made an incongruous sight. What the hotel proprietor thought of the arrangement, Karen couldn't begin to imagine. Providing he was being paid, she supposed he wouldn't be too disturbed by the vagaries of the clientele.

As the only non-British member of the party, Luz was something of an anomaly in himself. It seemed odd that an obviously well-educated man should choose to spend the major part of his life in this backwater of civilisation. If he had family in town, he would surely be spending the night with them while he still had the chance?

Lightly padded on the underside, the bed-roll was proving quite comfortable. Karen had plumped for the cotton pyjamas as the least likely to raise anyone's blood-pressure. Jake or no Jake, she refused to incarcerate herself in a brassière tomorrow. It would be sheer torture in this sticky heat. Her shirts were loose enough to conceal the lack, anyway.

Roger was already asleep. She could hear his gentle snoring from where she lay, combatting others from farther off. Jake was up at the far end of the veranda alongside Luz. She wondered if he too snored in his sleep. By all accounts, men were more prone to it than women.

Better get accustomed to it, she told herself. They were going to be spending a minimum of two weeks out there.

At which point she finally dozed off herself she couldn't afterwards be sure. One minute she was despairing of getting any sleep at all, the next she was opening her eyes to dim grey light and the sound of Roger's voice.

'The bathroom is free at present,' he advised as she threw back the mosquito net. 'I'd grab the chance while you can. After this, it's going to be river or lake.'

Either of which would be preferable right now, thought Karen wryly. Furnished with a couple of hand-bowls and an ancient shower, the hotel bathroom was on a par with the other toilet facilities. Others were already stirring. Getting up, she reached for the towel she had left to dry over the veranda rail.

The clean cotton shirt and trousers she was planning to wear were folded on top of her pack, along with the trainer-type boots she had been advised to bring. Even in the dry season they were likely to experience some rain. Footwear had to be of a kind that would dry off without hardening in the process. Blisters were not only undesirable from a comfort angle, but likely to become infected once the skin was broken.

There was no lock on the bathroom door. Karen decided against trying out the shower, and opted for a quick wash-down at one of the bowls. As it had the night before, the water ran cold and discoloured. The best that could be said of it was that it was wet.

Stripping off the pyjama jacket, she worked up as good a lather as she was likely to get from her tablet of soap, and slid the sponge over chest and shoulders. The humidity would get to her along with everyone else once the day got into its stride, but she could at least start off feeling reasonably comfortable.

Viewed through the damp-spotted mirror, her face looked drained of its normal healthy colour, though her eyes were bright enough. The light filtering in through the one small and grimy window hardly helped. Tying her hair back into the nape of her neck would help her stay cool—or at least cooler. Had she given it any real thought she might even have had it cut. Short hair was fashionable right now.

The opening of the door caught her in the act of drying herself. Jake made no attempt to back out again. He was wearing the same khaki cotton trousers he had worn the day before, and had a towel slung over one bare shoulder.

'There are others waiting to use this place,' he said. 'You've had your five minutes.'

Holding her towel across her front, Karen glared at him. 'You're doing this on purpose!' she accused.

His shrug spoke volumes. 'It's your choice to be here. Just don't expect any special privileges.' He eyed the towel with ironical expression. 'Why the sudden modesty? You're hiding nothing I haven't already seen.'

She stayed as she was, the spark in her eyes countering the fluttering nerves in her stomach. 'An episode I don't intend repeating. If you've any finer instincts left at all, you'll give me a moment to dress.'

For an instant, seeing the sudden glint in his own eyes, she thought she had overstepped the mark, then he nodded briefly. 'One minute.'

Karen waited until the door was closed before discarding the towel and reaching for the clean clothing she had brought in with her. She was fully clad inside thirty seconds, her hair raked through with hasty fingers. There would have been no time to apply make-up even if she had intended to use it.

Mike had joined Jake outside the door when she emerged. He looked her over approvingly.

'Worth waiting for, even without the trappings!'

Jake made no comment. Both men went into the bathroom together, leaving Karen to make her way back to the veranda.

Roger had his bed-roll already packed in a waterproof covering and fastened to the base of his pack with the straps provided for the purpose. He was wearing the same kind of khaki trousers as Jake, with the bottoms tucked into his socks. A bush shirt completed his outfit.

'No pith helmet?' joked Karen. 'I thought all directors on location wore one of those!'

'Only in the movies,' he grinned. 'We'll be sheltered from the sun for the most part.' He watched her fish out the bright yellow scarf from her pack and loop it under her hair. 'That looks good.'

'I'm not doing it for the look,' she returned, 'just practicality. Do we eat before we leave?'

'We'd better,' he said, somewhat to her relief. 'Miguel managed to rustle up a pretty good meal last night—or someone did. I'm not too sure what breakfast might consist of in these parts. Tortillas, probably. They seem to be the staple diet.'

She didn't care what, Karen told herself, providing it was edible. The way she felt at the moment, she could eat a horse!

Nigel and Howard were the last on their feet. Luz had disappeared. Gone, Roger said, to double-check their transport and supplies. They were to travel in two boats on the main river. That much Karen knew. Roughly two days away lay the lake from where they would head into the jungle proper, leaving the boats tied up for the return journey to Fuentas.

Consisting of the inevitable maize pancakes piled high with beans and topped with fried eggs, breakfast was both filling and tasty. They ate outside on the front veranda at a table set there for the purpose.

Viewing the slow-rolling river just a few yards distant, Karen knew a sense of excitement. This was only the first of many such ventures. Before the year was out she would have travelled round the world in Roger's wake. Eventually she hoped to step into the same vocational shoes. Female producers were still in a minority, but up and coming. She had given herself three years in which to achieve her aim. Twenty-seven sounded about right.

Luz was down at the jetty where the two motorised dug-outs in which they were to travel were still in the process of being loaded with supplies. So much for an early start. Time meant little to these people, thought Karen, viewing the faces of those who had gathered to watch proceedings. Each day was much like another. Hence the interest in what had to be a rare diversion.

She steeled herself to meet the appraising blue gaze as Jake joined them at the table. The scarf fastening back her hair drew a waspish smile.

'The flies are going to love that,' he observed. 'Yellow attracts them. Try one of your spare bootlaces instead.'

'I didn't bring any spares,' Karen confessed, and saw the dark brows draw together.

'As a supposedly experienced trekker I'd have thought you'd have had that item down on your list of essentials as a matter of course. Or do you normally rely on others in the party to supply your needs?'

'Everyone is allowed a mistake from time to time,' she returned with acerbity. 'Apart from the odd super-being among us, of course. No doubt *you* never forget anything!'

The sarcasm left him untouched. 'No doubt. I've a couple of spare pairs in my pack, always providing you don't mind black.'

'Bootlaces sound a bit utilitarian,' protested Roger. 'Surely there's something else you can use, Karen?'

'I've used laces before this,' she assured him. 'It doesn't matter what, providing it serves the purpose.'

'In which case the scarf was superfluous,' put in Jake maddeningly. He indicated the food still left on her plate. 'I'd eat up if I were you. It's the last substantial meal you're likely to get until we make camp.'

Mike and the other two men all came out together, bringing the aluminium carriers in which all film and camera and sound equipment was packed. The two boats would be travelling in close convoy; filming would take place on the water as well as on land. The eventual viewers would only ever see the one party, consisting of Jake, Luz and the two Indian porters, of course. Relatively few would give a thought to the camera crew following in their wake, and fewer still to the direction needed to make the whole thing gel.

Team-work, Karen told herself: that was what it was all about. And she was a part of that team.

The sun was well up and the heat steadily building by the time they were ready to leave. Down at the jetty, Jake got into the boat in which he would be travelling to reach for the pack already stashed and unzip one of the outer pockets.

Trust him to know exactly where each and every item was stored, thought Karen sourly, accepting the pair of laces he handed up to her. It wasn't just the colour of the scarf that had bugged him, she was pretty sure—it was the feminine touch. He was simply underlining his disapproval of her presence. Well, tough! She was here, and there was nothing he could do now to change that fact.

Exchanging scarf for lace was the work of a moment. On impulse, she tied the former round the nearest support post, from which it hung limply in the still and sultry air. That it wouldn't be there when she returned she didn't need telling. Anyone who wanted it was welcome to it.

'Let's go,' said Roger. 'We're behind time as it is.'

The dug-outs were roomy enough and surprisingly stable. Seated under the canvas awning covering half their boat-length, Karen could only admire the fortitude of those in the leading craft, which sported no shelter from the sun's heat at all.

Jake was right up front, dark hair glinting in the brilliant light, the sleeves of his shirt rolled to the elbows to reveal tautly muscled forearms. Immediately behind him, Luz looked equally fit. Two men of different races, yet with an empathy unmarred by the time that had passed since their last mission together. Two men, Karen mused, who were both self-sufficient—neither needing nor wanting commitment to anything other than their chosen lifestyle. There was something depressing in that thought.

Once out in the middle of the river, with the outboards opened up a little more, their passage created a welcome breeze. The banks had jungle growing right down to the edge, with no sign that Karen could see of man, although she knew that the slash and burn agriculture was still practised in the area.

Of wildlife there was no shortage: brilliant white egrets fishing in the shallows along the banks, big ridge-backed turtles swimming just below the surface of the water, troupes of monkeys half hidden amid the dense greenery.

Iguanas basked in the sun on branches overhanging the water, primeval in their scaly hides and reptilian heads. Some were almost six feet in length. Even the knowledge that they were harmless vegetarians did little to soften the impression created.

Camera on shoulder, Howard was in his element. Mike was absorbed, too, in recording the sounds. A pity they couldn't record the scents as well, reflected Karen, sniffing the air: like newly turned earth interlaced with fragrances too subtle to be tied down.

Jake would be doing voice-overs later to supplement the unrehearsed dialogue. He was, Karen saw, making notes as he went along. Neither he nor Luz seemed in any way affected by the intrusive presence of the camera.

As always, she herself noted down everything Roger said in relation to the job in hand, numbering and dating each page for reference. Later, during the editing process, those selfsame notes could prove invaluable. Ideas didn't always stick in the mind.

The mosquitoes were a constant irritation, although the repellent she had brought along helped to keep them at bay. Of them all, Nigel was the worst bitten. By the time they pulled in to the bank for lunch, his exposed skin was dotted with the reddened, itching lumps.

'I've always been susceptible,' he acknowledged wryly when Karen sympathised with him. 'Midges, gnats—you name it.'

'Try my repellent,' she offered. 'It seems to be working fairly well for me.'

'I put some on this morning,' he said. 'Although a different brand from this, I'll grant you.' He took the bottle from her with a smile. 'I'll give it a go.'

Consisting of cold tortillas left over from breakfast, with cheese and fruit, the meal was soon over. One of the Indians, whose name was Santino, heated water for coffee on a small portable stove. They would live off the land wherever possible, said Jake, and reserve most of the dried stores for a time when they might be needed. Anyone with faddy tastes was going to find themselves in dire straits, he added only half humorously.

If that was a dig at her, he needn't bother, thought Karen. She'd eat whatever was on offer. She had already tasted both snake and alligator, and found neither unpalatable. All it took was an open mind.

Twisting and turning, often almost doubling back on itself, the river twined like a snake itself. At times the banks crowded close enough for the brilliant colours of both bird and plant life to be spotted amid the bright green foliage; at others they were several hundred yards apart. At few places would it have been possible to land without resorting to the machetes carried by both Indians, due to the sheer density of the jungle growth.

It was still only mid-afternoon when they reached the place Luz had earmarked from memory as the place where they would make camp for the night. Santino and his companion, Juan, set to work with machetes to cut corozo palm fronds and swiftly construct shelters called *champas*, under which the bed-rolls were to be spread.

'In case of rain, I imagine,' said Roger when Karen remarked on the amount of trouble being taken. 'Those leaves look solid enough to keep out all but the heaviest.' He gave her a sympathetic glance as she ran a hand round the back of her neck to ease her collar away from her damp skin. 'Not exactly a comfortable climate, is it? Not that you look bad on it.'

'I feel like a wet rag,' she confessed. 'But then so, I'm sure, does everyone else.' Her eyes turned involuntarily in the direction of the man at present talking with Luz some short distance away. 'Apart from those two. They seem impervious to the heat.'

'More a case of just not letting it get to them,' Roger responded. 'Mind over matter, or some such. Wish I had the same resilience.' He studied her for a moment, expression reflective. 'Regretting it?'

'No way!' Her tone was emphatic. 'It would take a whole lot more than a little humidity to make me wish I'd stayed home. If I'd wanted a nice safe studio job I'd never have applied for this one in the first place. I knew from your work what it might entail. You're known throughout the industry as the Livingstone of the TV era.'

'So I'd heard.' His smile had a wry slant. 'My wife has another name for me: Wandering Willie, the man who's never there! She probably has a legitimate grouse. I'm away for weeks at a time.'

'So are other husbands with a career to follow,' returned Karen loyally. 'She must have realised when she married you what it was going to be like.'

'I wasn't into the documentary scene then. The main trouble is, she has no concept of nor interest in my job as a whole.' He added, 'Never marry on a purely emotional basis, Karen. Compatibility is just as vital to a good and lasting relationship. If I ever marry again, that will be the factor I'll be looking for.'

She eyed him questioningly. 'You've made up your mind, then?'

'Yes. As soon as I get back I'm suing for divorce. We'll have to come to some arrangement over James.' There was a pause, a subtle change of tone. 'Do you plan on having children yourself some day?'

Karen laughed and shrugged. 'I hadn't got round to thinking about it. Not before I had a husband, at any rate—and only then if I could combine motherhood with a career.'

'So no man in mind at present?'

She chose to turn a deaf ear to the small warning voice. 'I've had neither time nor opportunity these last few months to form any relationships.'

'I meant back home.'

'Hardly that either, considering I've only been home twice.'

'There must have been someone in your life at some time,' he persisted. 'Looking the way you do, you don't get to be twenty-four without leaving a few broken hearts in your wake!'

Karen laughed, refusing to take the comment seriously. 'I'm no *femme fatale*! I've had boyfriends, of course, but I've just never met anyone I could consider spending the rest of my life with.'

'Meaning you don't believe in divorce?'

'I didn't say that.' She hesitated, aware that this whole conversation was taking a track she didn't want to pursue. 'It has to depend on circumstances, doesn't it? With no experience to offer, I can hardly make any hard and fast rules. If I marry at all I'd hope to make a lasting thing of it, but who knows?'

'Where there's hope there's chance,' he said lightly. 'Just be sure you choose somebody who shares the same interests, that's all.'

He left the subject alone after that, much to her relief. She could be reading the signs all wrong, of course, but she was starting to doubt it. Roger was developing a regard for her that went beyond the purely professional, and she didn't want that to happen. Attractive as a man though he undoubtedly was, he aroused neither emotional nor physical response in her.

Not like Jake, came the reluctant admittance. She might detest the man, but he could still set her pulses hammering with a glance. If she hadn't fought her instincts the other night he would have made love to her. Even thinking about it now sent a tremor down her spine. It would have meant nothing beyond the temporary enjoyment to him, of course, but she knew herself incapable of formulating the same attitude. That was why she had to stay away from him.

Last night's threats had simply been meant to taunt her. He wouldn't be following them up. What he would be doing was keeping a weather eye open for any sign of encouragement on her part when it came to others in the party. If there was discord at all it wasn't going to be her doing. She would make sure of that.

CHAPTER SIX

ALL around the clearing, the jungle closed in tightly. Others had camped here since Luz had last visited the site, Karen realised, seeing the darkened patch where a fire had recently smouldered.

Their own fire was laid and lit in the same spot, and the fish hooked by Santino within minutes of landing were spitted on sharp sticks to roast slowly over the glowing embers. Howard filmed the process. Bare seconds of the scene might eventually be used, or perhaps none of it at all, dependent on Roger's final concept. They had a long way to go as yet, and a whole lot of material to come.

Sunset brought a brief dusk, turning the trees to blue and then to black. With bird calls stilled, the forest was far from silent. The cicadas alone filled the air with sound. A sudden ear-splitting cacophony turned out to be caused by howler monkeys. They would be repeating the performance at dawn, it appeared, or at any time during the night too if their domain was threatened.

Conversation was desultory. Karen listened with half an ear, joining in only where she felt she had something useful to contribute. Lit by fireglow, the male faces about her looked a uniform colour, though obviously differing in bone-structure. If Mike wasn't careful he would be running to fat in a very few years' time, she thought dispassionately. The evidence was already there in the softening of his jawline and hint of jowls to come.

Of them all, Howard was the only one with what could rightly be called a life outside his work, although he never mentioned his family. Two separate existences, she assumed. His wife must be a very understanding and tolerant woman.

Catching Nigel's eye, she flashed an automatic smile. He and Howard were as different as chalk from cheese, yet they obviously got along fine. There were times when she felt almost motherly towards him, despite his two years' seniority. Wet behind the ears, her father would have called him.

She realised suddenly that Jake was watching her from across the far side of the fire. The dancing light played over strong cheekbones, outlining the cynically slanted mouth. Her heart performed its fast becoming familiar double beat before settling back to a steady rhythm. Damn the man! she thought fiercely. Why did he have to be here, spoiling this for her?

Was that what she really meant? came the sneaking question. Would she really prefer his absence to his presence—or was that simply the voice of self-preservation?

The fish proved delicious. They would be following a water course from the lake, albeit a much smaller one than this, so food shouldn't be a problem. There were other edible forms of game to be found in the jungle too. Luz was packing a rifle. To be used only in the procurement of food, he had said. Karen wondered if that rule would hold fast should they be confronted by anything dangerous. Jaguars were reputedly shy of man, but there was always the exception.

Tired after the long day, she was no more loath than anyone else to retire for the night. Whether by accident or design, Jake was right next door, with Luz on her far side.

Clad once again in the confining pyjamas, Karen envied the men their freedom of apparel. The heat and humidity had scarcely diminished with the onset of night. Even rain would be welcome.

'It's going to get worse before it gets better,' said Jake softly, as if sensing her discomfort. 'You wanted to come.'

'So, who's complaining?' she hissed. 'I'm fine, thanks!'

'Of course you are.' His voice was heavy with irony. 'You're prepared to lie your head off rather than admit you might have made a mistake. Just remember there's no turning back.'

I wouldn't even if I could, she was on the verge of declaring, but she bit it back. One could protest too much. 'Goodnight,' she said pointedly instead.

He made no answer. Lying there, cocooned in filmy muslin, she felt cut off in more ways than one. There was an ache inside her that wouldn't go away.

She was woken several times in the night by various unfamiliar sounds. Once it was to see the fire being replenished with wood by Luz. There was no movement from Jake—no snoring either, although she lay for some time listening for it. When she finally fell asleep again it was to dream of Mayan temples and sacrificial altars, of cruel-eyed men dressed in jaguar skins and quetzal feathers. It was no coincidence that they all looked like Jake Rothman.

The howler monkeys roused them at dawn with a screaming chorus that must be audible twenty miles away. Desperate for a wash, Karen filled a pan with water and found a spot where she could sponge herself down in private before donning a clean shirt.

She had rinsed yesterday's things through before retiring, and hung them to dry under the *champa*. If she continued to do that each evening she could cope well enough, she thought now, packing the clean, if creased, items away.

Apart from Mike, who had declared his intention of growing a beard, and the Indians, who didn't need to, all the men had shaved. Of them all, it was Mike who looked the worse for wear.

'Hardly slept a wink,' he groused. 'Damned mosquitoes got through regardless.' He indicated the telltale red swellings on his arms. 'I'm bitten to death!'

Karen had been bitten herself, though not badly. The repellent she was using was fortunately odourless to the human olfactory senses, but the insects didn't seem to like it much. She considered offering Mike the use of it, dismissing the idea because she was likely to run out altogether if she did so. There were times when self-interest had to come first. Like them all, he had received the necessary inoculations and was taking anti-malarial tablets. Apart from the discomfort, he should come to no lasting harm.

Nigel was another matter. In addition to the mosquitoes, he had also been attacked by ticks. These Luz had removed for him, but the welts left behind must itch like fury. There would be enough of her repellent for the two of them if they were reasonably careful, Karen calculated. She ensured no one else was watching when she offered him one of her two bottles of the stuff after they'd eaten.

'Are you sure you can spare it?' he asked with ill-concealed reluctance to turn the offer down. 'It certainly seemed to work yesterday.'

'Just eke it out a little,' she advised. 'We'll manage.'

'Thanks.' His gratitude was unfeigned. 'You're a real brick, Karen!'

Not exactly a flattering description, she thought amusedly, but the sentiment was genuine.

'If you two are quite ready, we're leaving,' said Jake, making her start because she hadn't seen him approaching. The narrowed regard shifted from her to Nigel and back again, losing nothing of its hardness in the process. 'You still have to pack your bed-roll—or were you expecting someone to do it for you?'

'Of course not,' she denied. 'It won't take me a moment.'

'I'll help you,' offered the younger man.

'No, you won't.' Jake spoke quietly but firmly. 'On this trip we handle our own gear. You've got three minutes,' he added to Karen. 'What you don't have on board by then we leave. Clear?'

'As crystal.' She made no attempt to keep the bite from her voice. 'I was under the impression that Luz was leading the party.'

'Guiding,' he corrected. 'There's no leader as such.'

'Is that a fact?' She was moving as she spoke, passing him by with heart beating fast and hard in her throat, conscious of the compression about the strong mouth and the not too remote a chance that, Nigel or no Nigel, he might feel moved to press the message home with some rather more physical gesture. 'I'll bear it in mind.'

Everyone else was down at the water's edge if not already on board the craft when she got there. Roger accepted her apology for keeping them all waiting with a dismissive shrug.

'A few minutes isn't going to matter much,' he said. 'We'll be spending enough time cramped up in there as it is.'

'You'll have chance to stretch your legs after we reach the lake,' said Luz. 'We have a lot of jungle to get through before we find what we're looking for.'

'*If* we find it.' Mike sounded less than cheerful over the prospect. 'I hadn't realised just how dense this stuff would be!'

'One reason why Santino and Juan and I have machetes,' came the smooth reply. 'We'll clear a path for you. As to finding the place again, all we have to do is follow the compass course I took the first time.'

Considering the heaviness of the undergrowth, Karen doubted if it was going to be quite as simple as he made it sound. So long as she wasn't expected to wield a machete, however, she would battle through. There really wasn't any choice.

The day passed in much the same way as the one previous. Not that Karen felt she could ever grow bored with the passing scene. There was nothing regimented about the Petan jungle. The variety of trees alone was unexpected.

They reached the convergence of the smaller river on which the lake was situated mid-afternoon. The current here was stronger and against them, but nothing the outboards couldn't cope with. Unlike the main river, where the banks were sometimes several hundred yards apart, these were no more than twenty or thirty feet away, creating a faintly claustrophobic atmosphere. Although she rarely actually saw anything, the occasional heavy splash and spread of ripples from the shallows was suggestive enough to send ripples along Karen's spine.

She was glad to reach the lake with its promise of rest and refreshment before the foot-slog to come tomorrow. Caused by the river flow's re-routing itself across the neck of a bend at some time in the distant past, it was shaped like a bow, with the widest point no more than three hundred yards across. The water within the arc of the bow was as smooth as glass.

Luz directed them to a spot where the land sloped down to the water's edge and was relatively clear of undergrowth. That they weren't the first here either became evident when they saw the remains of a thatched-roof hut at the rear of the sizeable clearing.

Left from the days when old-time loggers employed spotters to seek out the valuable mahogany trees dispersed throughout the forest, explained Luz. Any spotting done today was from aircraft capable of flying low enough to pinpoint the distinctive spreading crown of dark-green leathery leaves.

Champas were built and a fire laid. Juan, Mike and Nigel took one of the boats out on to the lake to fish for supper, while Luz and Santino disappeared into the forest in search of other game.

Karen found herself a seat on a convenient log and watched the flocks of snowy white egrets flying in to roost in a dead tree on the opposite shore. Squabbling and jostling like schoolboys on an outing, they filled every branch, until the whole tree looked as if it were covered in huge blossoms. Behind them, the sky turned from pink to red and began deepening towards the purple of dusk.

Howard was recording it all, but she wished she had brought a camera of her own along too. For the first time she could begin to appreciate what it was that had made Jake seek a lifestyle where scenes such as these were on regular offer. Not for him the tedious day-to-day routine of an office.

Her pulse went into overdrive as someone came up behind her. She didn't need to turn her head to know who the newcomer was; her every sense was alert to his presence.

'Something I should be doing instead of lazing around?' she asked.

'Nothing I can think of at the moment.' Jake stepped over the log to take a seat at her side, resting an arm along his knee as he looked out across the lake. 'An exceptional sight,' he remarked. 'One of those times that makes it all worthwhile.'

'I'd have thought it was *all* worthwhile to you,' said Karen softly, and steeled herself, for the gaze turned her way.

'There's always the rough along with the smooth, whatever the job.'

'I'm finding that out for myself,' she acknowledged. 'Is it likely to get any rougher?'

Blue eyes registered the gibe with a glint. 'That depends on your concept of rough. Taking a singular interest in young Nigel the way you were doing this morning isn't likely to help matters.'

'*Young* Nigel,' she retorted, 'is twenty-six years old!'

'There's more to age than mere years.'

'How very profound.'

Jake gave her a calculated look. 'Are you trying to goad me? If so, you're doing a fine job. It's obvious to anybody with the eyes to see it that Morris is well and truly smitten. You're not doing him any favours by encouraging his hopes for a closer relationship.'

'I offered him the use of my insect repellent, not my body,' Karen returned levelly. 'If that constitutes encouragement in your book, then you have a warped mind. About Nigel's feelings I wouldn't know. Unlike some, I——'

'You know.' The statement was flat. 'A woman always knows when a man has the hots for her.'

Her teeth came together hard. It took all she had to keep her voice low. 'It's usually the inarticulate who need to fall back on crudity to express themselves. I'd have thought your vocabulary a little more extensive.'

'Oh, it is.' He was unmoved by the slur. 'It just happens to be a very good description of what happens to a man when he talks with or looks at a woman he wants to make love to. There are other physiological symptoms too, of course, but I'm sure I don't need to underline those. Right this minute I've more of an inclination towards violence than ardour myself, although the two can come pretty close. Just keep a rein on that tongue of yours if you want to survive this trip.'

'I'll make a pact with you,' she said huskily. 'You leave me alone, and I'll leave you alone!'

'But will you leave the others alone?' He shook his head, the line of his mouth mocking her impotent anger. 'You're typical of the species, Karen. Light the touch paper, then stand back and wait for the explosion!'

It took her a moment or two to form a reply. When she did speak it was with heavy irony. 'You must have been very badly hurt by some woman to make you so bitter.'

His laugh was short. 'I'm not bitter, simply realistic. The best way to avert trouble would be for one of us to lay prior claim, so to speak.'

'With yourself as prime candidate, no doubt!'

He inclined his head. 'I've hardly made any secret of the fact that I want you. It started the minute you walked up those steps back at the house and gave me that green-eyed glare. Here, I thought, is a woman who badly needs putting down—in the very finest sense, of course.'

Both Karen's hands had balled into tight little fists, the nails cutting into her palms; she could feel herself trembling both inwardly and outwardly. 'You're depraved—do you know that?' she spat at him.

'Deprived would be closer. If you want the truth, I've never stopped kicking myself for turning down what you were offering the other night.'

'An aberration on my part,' she responded with force. 'You can be sure it won't be happening again!'

'Now there's an interesting challenge.' His voice was taunting. 'What was it you said about human failings?' He got to his feet in one lithe movement, looking down at her with a suddenly sombre expression. 'We've a long way to go yet. A lot of things could happen.'

Not the kind of things *he* was talking about, Karen thought vehemently as he moved away. She would be giving him no opportunity to carry out the implied threat.

Roger cornered her after supper, ostensibly to discuss the day's work, although it soon became obvious that his heart, for once, wasn't really in it.

'What were you and Jake talking about so intently earlier?' he asked with apparent casualness eventually. 'You looked ready to do him a serious injury when he came away.'

Karen kept her tone equally casual. 'Just a reiteration of the same old theme. It gets a bit wearing, that's all.'

'Seems he's not about to let you forget you're here under sufferance.' Roger added swiftly, 'His, that is, not mine. Are you sorry you came? The comfort level isn't exactly high.'

She shook her head emphatically. 'I'm not in the least bit sorry. The comfort level is no worse than I've experienced before.'

'Even the heat and the flying stock?'

She laughed and shrugged. 'Well, maybe a little worse. The point is, I can stand it. I can stand anything I'm called on to undergo—anything *any* of us is called on to undergo. All I ask is to be treated as just one of the unit.'

It was Roger's turn to smile. 'I have to admit it isn't that easy. I suppose Jake had a point. Bringing a woman along on this kind of project was bound to cause complications. I didn't give it enough thought in the beginning.'

Karen eyed him questioningly. 'You mean you'd as soon I hadn't followed you to San Samoza?'

'In some respects, not in others.' He hesitated a moment before adding slowly, 'You have to know how I feel about you, Karen. It isn't just a working relationship. Not for me. I thought, perhaps, not wholly for you either?'

Her heart sank. This was all she needed! Looking back, she supposed she had suspected something of the kind all along. Turning a blind eye was all too easy. Faced with the actuality, she scarcely knew what to say for the best.

'Roger——' she began, but he held up a staying hand.

'Look, I realise this isn't the best of times, so let's leave it there for the moment, shall we? I just wanted to be sure you were aware, that's all.' He touched her hand. 'OK?'

The time was right here and right now, but she couldn't bring herself to make the move. For him to believe her even remotely interested in a closer relationship, she must have given some impression, no matter how inadvertently, of that desire. Telling him how wrong he was was hardly going to improve the present situation. It would have to wait.

She forced a smile. 'OK.'

Jake was talking with Luz some distance away. Roger went to join them, leaving Karen to contemplate a future no longer as bright as it had been some minutes ago. It would be difficult, to say the least, to go on working with Roger after this, yet where else was she to find a job like this one? It was becoming apparent that Jake might have had a valid point in saying Roger had been swayed as much by her personal appeal for him as her ability to fill the post, much as she hated to acknowledge it.

Somewhere back in the forest an owl began calling: a deep and resonant hooting that was nothing like the 'to-whit, to-whoo' of popular fiction. Other sounds were silenced for an instant, and then started again.

The rustling in the trees could have been caused by wind, except that the air was so oppressively still. Monkeys, or whatever; it was unlikely, Karen assured herself, that anything threatening lurked out there. All the same, she was thankful not to be alone.

They were all in their sleeping bags before ten o'clock. This time Karen was flanked by Howard and Luz. Whether it had been Jake's own choice to distance himself from her, or simply a matter of chance, she couldn't be sure. The fact that he *was* some distance away was all that mattered to her.

Apart from the glow from the fire, it was still pitch-dark when she awoke. The luminous face of her watch told her it was only two-thirty in the morning. No one else was stirring. Even sitting in a boat all day could still take its toll.

After less than five hours' sleep Karen would have expected to feel tired still herself, but she didn't. There was a restlessness inside her that wouldn't be repressed. Lying there in the sleeping bag under the enveloping net, she felt trapped.

Eventually, unable to stand it any longer, she eased herself carefully out. The damp heat slicked her body in perspiration. All that water out there was a real temptation. She could be in and out again in moments.

Pausing only to pull on her boots, she crept out from under the *champa* as silently as she could. Her eyes were beginning to adjust to the darkness now. Providing she didn't look directly at the fire, she could see well enough to pick her way across the camp-site and down the slope to the water's edge where the boats were moored.

She was out of sight of the casual observer now. Swiftly stripping off the pyjamas, she draped both items over a convenient branch and stood for a moment, savouring the relative coolness on her bare skin before taking a tentative step towards the water. A quick dip and out again; she wouldn't risk a swim.

The bare arm, whipped around her waist from the rear, shocked the life out of her. For an awful second she thought it was a boa constrictor that had a grip on her. Only when she was brought up hard against the obviously human body did terror loose its hold on her.

'What the hell do you think you're doing?' Jake gritted in her ear.

'What do *you* think I'm doing?' Karen snapped back. She tore at the arm still clasped about her waist, not caring whether she drew blood in her sudden frenzy. 'Let go of me!'

He spun her around instead, holding her so close that she had to lean back against the confining arm to see the dark face looming over her. 'You little fool,' he clipped. 'Have you any idea what could have happened to you out there?'

'I wasn't planning on going far out,' she denied. 'Or for long enough to be in any danger.'

'Piranha don't hang about. They can strip a horse to the bone in minutes. Given flesh as tender as yours, I'd say bare seconds would be enough.' His gaze dropped to her naked breasts, taking on some new expression in the process. 'You'd have made a rare feast.'

'If it was as dangerous as all that I'm quite sure you'd have said something before this,' she shot at him, refusing to flinch from his regard.

'I credited you with enough common sense,' he came back. 'Seems I was wrong. You don't even listen to reason. Just because you've so far seen nothing of any great note out here don't run away with the idea that danger doesn't exist. Once we're on foot it's going to be ever present. Snakes will usually get out of your way if they hear you coming, but there are exceptions. The bushmaster, for instance, can be downright aggressive if it considers its territory is being violated.'

Regardless of the futility in such an action, it was taking her all her time to resist the urge to put an arm across her chest. She felt totally vulnerable.

'You made your point,' she said jerkily. 'Now will you please let me go?'

'I didn't even start making my point,' he returned on a grim note. 'I don't think you've heard a word I've said! What does it take to get through to you?'

'I heard,' she confirmed. 'I shan't be taking any more risks, don't worry. Not that I consider the wildlife the real menace round here!'

In this light the blue eyes looked black, with glittering pinpoints like stars in a night sky. 'You just don't know where to draw the line, do you?' he said softly. 'Or is the aggro deliberate?'

She stared at him, shaken by the suspicion that he was probably right. She wanted him to retaliate, to kiss her again—to give her no other choice but to go along with whatever he wanted to do to her. Liking or not liking had nothing to do with it.

'That's ridiculous!' she forced out.

'Is it?' His voice had roughened again. 'Let's find out, shall we?'

CHAPTER SEVEN

KAREN put up some pretence of a struggle as Jake pulled her to him, but it was only a token gesture, and they both knew it. His mouth was demanding but not harsh, seeking and gaining response. Dissenting voices blanked out, she slid her arms about his neck and gave herself over to the incredible sensation of naked flesh against naked flesh, moaning deep in her throat as his tongue parted her lips with such delicate yet irresistible insistence.

She had known from the beginning that it could be like this with him, although nothing in her life before had prepared her for the sheer intensity of desire. Even if she had wanted to stop she would have been incapable of making her physical being obey her will. And she didn't want to stop. She didn't want ever to stop!

The feel of his hand at her breast was exquisite, his lips even more so. His tongue was a flickering torment, making her writhe in his arms even as she clutched the dark head close. Awareness of where they were, of others in such relative proximity, had vanished along with the last glimmer of personal restraint. Tomorrow didn't matter; only tonight.

She went down under him readily, welcoming the hard weight of his body. There had been no other man in her life who could make her feel this way. It was like being released from prison. Jake Rothman, so strong, so vital; so utterly and completely male!

The trembling as he explored her started deep, building to a crescendo that shook her whole body as he took control of her inner being.

'That was for you,' he said softly in her ear. 'This is for both of us...'

Karen closed her eyes when he finally moved over her again, though not in fear. The sensation as they came together was incredible. She felt his hand across her mouth, choking off the involuntary cry; remaining there as he began the strong, possessive movements her whole body craved.

And she was answering that call with equal fervour, biting into the stretched fingers in a mounting frenzy of emotion until everything blurred and fell away, and there was nothing left but an empty shell.

How long they lay there she couldn't have said. Coming back to life and slowly dawning realisation was painful. There could be no going back from here. She was stuck with the situation she herself had precipitated. What Jake was thinking and feeling at this moment she hardly dared to contemplate. Satisfaction allied to contempt, at a guess.

'If I said I was sorry that happened I'd be a liar,' he murmured. 'It had to come sooner or later.' He levered himself up on an elbow to look down into her shadowed face, his own expression unrevealing. 'You weren't exactly unwilling.'

'You don't need to underline it,' she said huskily. 'I feel bad enough already.'

Jake cocked his head to one side. 'You didn't enjoy it?'

Karen could feel the hot wave of colour washing over her, and was thankful for the darkness concealing it. 'I don't want to talk about it,' she gritted through clenched teeth. 'Just let me go, Jake.'

'You'd as soon forget it, is that what you're saying?' He sounded suddenly grim. 'Well, tough. I already told you I wasn't prepared to play that kind of game. Having had you once, I'm going to want you again. A fact of life. We can't just walk away from it now.'

'We can't just carry on with it either,' she said desperately. 'What if...the others found out?'

'Meaning Roger in particular?' He was watching her face, eyes well enough adjusted to catch her fleeting change of expression. 'Exactly what plans do you have in that direction?'

'Professional ones only. I've already told you that.'

'Hardly his own view of the future. You're the reason his marriage is on the rocks.'

'That's not true!' She was incensed by the injustice of the accusation. 'It was over long before I came on the scene.'

'Then you put the final nail in the coffin.'

'Not that either. I've never knowingly offered him the least encouragement.'

'Knowingly or unknowingly, you've given him some cause to believe you feel something for him outside work. He sounded sure enough of it earlier when he warned me off.'

'Warned you off?' Karen had stiffened. She added slowly, 'Is that the reason for...what just happened?'

The strong mouth pulled into a brief and cynical smile. He ran his eyes down the length of her body, paler than the ground on which she lay. 'The reason for what just happened, as you so delicately put it, is right here. It would have taken a saint to resist the temptation, and I've no pretences in that direction. If you mean what you say about Roger you'll make things clear to him. If you don't I'll do it for you.'

Karen gazed up into the unyielding features, wondering how she could feel anything at all beyond hatred for this man. 'You'd tell him about this?'

'If necessary. It might be too late to save his marriage, but he deserves better than to be used as a mere stepping-stone. If you have the talent you'll make it anyway.' He rolled away from her to sit up and reach for the shorts he had discarded. 'We'd better get back before we're missed. It wouldn't do to cause dissension in camp.'

'I despise you!' Her voice trembled. 'I really despise you!'

'No, you don't.' He said it quite matter-of-factly. 'You feel the same way about me as I do about you—and we haven't got it out of our systems yet by a long chalk. Whether we will have by the time we get back to base remains to be seen.'

Karen sat up herself, too well aware that her own items of clothing were out of immediate reach. 'This won't be happening again,' she stated with hard-won control. 'I can promise you that!'

'You said that before,' Jake reminded her softly. 'No doubt you'll say it several times more before we're through. Women always like to believe they're more capable than men of repressing their baser impulses, no matter how many times they're proved wrong. I'll keep my back turned while you dress, by the way, if that's what's bothering you. Far be it from me to embarrass a lady.'

The satire cut where it was intended. Even without the darkness to cloak her movements, the events of the last half-hour or so made modesty a bit meaningless. Her legs felt rubbery when she stood. She dusted off the debris sticking to her back as best she could before donning the pyjamas again.

'You go first,' Jake invited. 'I'll wait a while. Less risk of waking everyone up.'

Karen doubted whether he would care over-much if anyone did see the two of them returning to camp together. No matter what he said, it was different for a man. Making love with Jake had been wonderful while it had lasted, but she still felt sullied. The thought of facing any of the others, knowing that they knew, was anathema to her.

People who couldn't stand the heat should stay out of the kitchen, she reflected painfully as she turned without another word to make her way back to the *champas*. She just wasn't cut out for this kind of thing. Jake had undermined every principle she held dear, and without hardly trying. That he could do it again, given half a chance, she could no longer afford to doubt. So she had to make sure he never had that chance, didn't she? Even if everything in her cried out to be with him.

The fire had burned low. She paused to put on some more of the wood lying ready for the purpose before gliding across to slide under the *champa* and into her sleeping-bag. Howard was breathing deeply and evenly on her right, the rest of the sleepers equally at rest, so far as she could tell.

Only when she turned on to her side did she see that Luz's eyes were open, reflecting the light from the newly replenished fire. There was no censure in them, just a measured scrutiny, but she was sure that he knew what had been going on. She conquered with an effort the urge to say something in mitigation. For one thing, it wasn't his business, and for another there was nothing she *could* say that would make any difference.

She heard Jake coming back some minutes later, for the simple reason that she was still awake—and likely to remain so. If either of his two immediate neighbours were awoken by his movements they would probably assume that he had simply been answering a call of nature.

Which he had, of course, came the wry thought, if in a rather different sense. Lying here now, she wanted him with an intensity that hurt. Hate and love were close cousins, it was said, but she didn't believe it. She dared not allow herself to believe it.

Morning found her unrefreshed both in body and spirit. She couldn't bring herself to meet Jake's eyes straight on, afraid of what she might see in them. A strip wash, using water drawn from the river, went some way towards improving her outlook on life. Wearing a clean shirt and trousers, she felt ready, if not exactly eager, to face whatever the day might bring.

They left the boats securely moored. Short of being swamped in one of the heavier tropical downpours—unlikely at this time of the year—they should be safe enough until their return. The thought of the journey which lay ahead gave Karen her first real taste of trepidation. With piranha in the water and snakes on land, the chances of being bitten by one or the other seemed suddenly less than remote.

To her untutored eyes, the jungle backing the clearing all looked equally impenetrable, but Luz seemed able to pick out the beginnings of a trail of sorts. Unsheathing his machete, Santino began hacking his way into the wall of greenery, slicing through palm fronds and lianas with deceptive ease. Shirt already soaked beneath the clinging weight of her backpack, Karen could only be thankful that she didn't have to do anything more strenuous than follow in his wake.

The undergrowth thinned out a short distance in, which made the going easier. Birds screeched warnings overhead, although it was difficult to spot them at first in the leafy canopy. Only as her eyes became accustomed to the dappling of light and shade did Karen begin to see something of the teeming jungle life.

Her first glimpse of humming birds hovering over the purple, trumpet-like flowers of a morning glory brought a gasp of sheer delight. Gauzy wings shimmering, bodies shot with all the colours of the rainbow, they were exquisite little creatures.

Howard got the scene on camera. He was filming the lead party intermittently under Roger's direction, with Mike recording Jake's observations. From time to time, where something of note occurred, they would be setting up static sessions too, but wildlife shots had for the most part to depend on luck, due to their limited time. The detailed encounters, as Jake himself said, were Attenborough's province.

They heard the river before they reached it. Both too narrow and too shallow to be navigable by the dug-outs, Karen saw, although canoes might have managed it.

'How long is it going to take us to reach this site, do you think?' she asked Roger as the party took a break before beginning to follow the course upstream.

'Depends how it goes,' he returned. 'Luz says two days, but that's assuming he can find the place again without difficulty. This river apparently runs from another lake close by the site, so it shouldn't prove too difficult. Petan is riddled with water-holes of one kind or another. I imagine that was one reason why the Maya chose to build their cities here in the first place.' He gave her an oblique glance. 'Have you thought about what I said yesterday?'

'I thought we were going to forget all that until after this is over,' she got out.

'That was the idea,' he admitted, 'only I'm finding it impossible. I need an answer. Or at least some kind of reassurance. How *do* you feel about me?'

Jake was close by, discussing something with Luz. She kept her voice low. 'I admire and respect you, Roger, but that's as far as it goes. I'm sorry if I've given you any other impression. It wasn't intentional.'

'I see.' His face had darkened. 'You mean I've been reading too much into too little?'

'Something like that, I suppose.' She made a helpless little gesture. 'I honestly didn't realise you were thinking that way. If I had——'

'If you had you'd have what?' he asked as her voice petered out. 'Given up the job?'

Karen bit her lip. 'I don't know. I imagine it's immaterial now, anyway.'

He shot her another glance. 'And what exactly is that supposed to mean?'

'It has to be obvious that I have to find another job once we get back.'

'Because of this?' He shook his head. 'I can live with it if you can.'

'But it would always be there,' she protested.

'My problem.' His voice was matter-of-fact. 'This is one time when personal interests have to be put aside. I'd have a hard job finding another assistant as good as you've turned out to be—especially one as willing to take the rough along with the smooth the way you are.'

Karen said hesitantly, 'Shall you still be going in for a divorce when we get back?'

He shrugged. 'Probably. I need to cut loose from Sylvia.'

'And James?'

'I'd be granted reasonable access. I see little enough of him as it is.'

Jake was on his feet, along with the rest of the party. The glance he cast their way was narrowed. 'Ready to go?'

'As ready as we'll ever be,' replied Roger lightly. He got up from the tree stump and offered Karen a helping hand, looking into her eyes with a reassuring smile. 'The job comes first.'

That she could believe. If Sylvia knew it too, which no doubt she did, could one blame her too much for seeking solace elsewhere?

The day went through its phases, hot and sticky, yet not without compensations. There was so much to see, so much to film—some of it with the human element on camera, some without.

Without Jake, many creatures of the forest would have gone unnoted. He was the one who spotted the tiny bright red frog from which South American Indians used to obtain the poison with which they tipped their blowpipe darts; the colony of leaf-cutting ants carrying their slices of greenery like banners in a parade; the pair of scarlet macaws half hidden on a tree branch.

Birds and butterflies abounded. One of the latter, with a five-inch wing-span, had huge spots like eyes on its wings. Karen was unsurprised to find it was called the owl butterfly.

The undergrowth was thickest where the sun's rays could penetrate the canopy above, but in the shadier areas the ground between the trees was relatively clear. Hardly Tarzan's kind of jungle, as Jake remarked. The lianas festooning the trees were not made for swinging on, except perhaps by monkeys.

They made camp for the night in a natural clearing some short distance away from the river they were more or less following. Drawn by the sound of rushing water, Karen discovered a small fall, with a pool below that was big enough and looked deep enough for swimming in. Hot as she was, the thought of piranha was deterrent enough.

She stiffened as Jake joined her at the water's edge, too reminiscent of last night—although at least she was fully dressed this time.

'It's all right,' she said. 'I'm not about to sacrifice myself.'

'I came to tell you there's little danger of finding piranha here,' he returned expressionlessly. 'Luz gives the place a clean bill of health. The rest of us can bathe *en masse*. If you're going to go in I'd suggest you do it now.'

'While you watch?' She shook her head. 'Thanks, but no, thanks. I'll wait my turn.'

'If I stayed around it would be as a safeguard against anything untoward happening—no other reason,' he said. 'I'm no voyeur.' Hands thrust into trouser pockets, he added levelly, 'I'm not making any apologies for what happened last night. You had it coming.'

She drew in a ragged breath. 'Retaliation is what we're talking about.'

'There might have been an element of that in it to start with.' He was looking at the water, not at her, a faint smile etching his lips. 'The rest was pure need. Have you got round to putting Roger straight yet?'

'I keep telling you, there's nothing to put straight.'

'And I say there is.' The smile was still there, but different. 'So, it's going to be up to me.'

'It doesn't have anything to do with you,' she responded desperately. 'Jake——'

'You can have half an hour on your own in the water,' he cut in imperturbably. 'That includes fetching your things, so I'd get moving if I were you. I'll wait here till you get back, and act as look-out. That is, unless you'd prefer Mike or Nigel, say, to do the honours?'

'I'd as soon not have anyone,' she said, abandoning her attempt to reason with him. 'There's little difference between one snake in the grass and another!'

His laugh held genuine amusement. 'I wouldn't bet on it.'

Getting at him that way was a waste of time, Karen conceded, turning away to start back to camp. And he was right, of course. If it came to a choice she would rather have him looking out for her safety than any of the others.

The memory of what he had said about last night brought mixed emotions. Pure need, he had called it. Well, yes, she could go along with that too. Only on her side there had been factors additional to the physical aspect—there still were. Somewhere under that case-hardened exterior lay a man she wanted to know better. She had caught glimpses of him when he talked about his work; had seen the tender sensitivity in those lean brown hands when he touched a plant. Trying to score points off him wasn't going to get her anywhere. If she wanted him to change his attitude then she had to change hers.

As to where exactly she wanted to get with Jake she wasn't at all sure. After last night she wasn't too sure about anything beyond the fact that she would never forget him.

She managed to pick up her things without attracting attention from any of the others, who were all busy in various ways. It was only a matter of a couple of hundred yards or so back to the river, and not a difficult path to tread, owing to the scanty undergrowth. All the same, Karen took care to watch where she was putting her feet. A curled bushmaster could look like a pile of dead leaves until disturbed; she had already seen one such snake pointed out by Luz. They were carrying antidote, of course, but there was no point in taking unnecessary risks.

Jake was sitting on a long slab of rock she hadn't noticed on her previous visit to the river pool. Seeing the tangle of grasses and vines around it, she concluded that he must have discovered and uncovered it while she had been gone. Only when he rose and beckoned her over did she realise that the slab had a pattern of hieroglyphics carved into its upper face.

'A Maya stela,' said Jake. 'Lord knows how and why it's here. There don't seem to be any others around.'

Karen put out a tentative hand to trace the faint figuring, shivering deep inside at the thought of the centuries that had passed since these carvings had been done. According to what Luz had said, they were still a couple of days' travel from the site he had discovered, so this could hardly be a part of it.

'Could it have been a kind of memorial to someone who perhaps died at this spot?' she asked hesitantly, preparing herself for ridicule from the master. 'These things were monuments to the Maya leaders, weren't they?'

'That's right.' Jake's gaze held no hint of scorn. 'As I said before, you've done your homework. It's a possibility, although not a common occurrence.'

The concordance brought a pleasurable glow. She said quickly, 'I'm a rank amateur, but I find the whole thing fascinating. Why do *you* think the Maya civilisation ended so abruptly?'

His shrug was good-humoured. 'Your guess is as good as mine. Disease, famine, drought; maybe even social revolution when the commoners got tired of being used as a combination of slave labour and sacrificial lambs. If I had to make a single choice I'd come down on the side of that last theory. It makes sense.'

It appealed to Karen too, though she refrained from saying so. Opinions based on nothing more concrete than a feeling were worthless. Talking with Jake like this elicited feelings of a different kind. She wanted the moment to last. If only, she thought wryly, she were capable of meeting him on the same level. He was so clever, so knowledgeable. No amount of reading could equip her for informed discussion.

A line was drawn between the dark brows as he studied her. He seemed to be debating with himself. When he spoke again it was on a new and faintly rueful note.

'You're a disturbing influence, Karen.'

She said huskily, 'I don't mean to be.'

'Mean it or not, you've become a headache I could have done without. I keep seeing you the way you were last night—feeling you under me, so smooth and silky and responsive. I've never——'

'Don't.' Her voice was ragged. 'Jake, about last night——' she paused, searching for the right words, finding only the trite reaffirmation '—I didn't intend things to happen that way.'

'I didn't follow you with that in mind either,' he said, then gave a dry little smile. 'At least, not consciously. I didn't do myself any long-term favours in giving way to the impulse either. I've a feeling I'm going to be spending a few sleepless nights over you.'

Karen had a certainty that she would be spending more than a few herself, and not just for a short period. Looking at him now, she was shaken by the sudden tumult of emotion. Where else was she going to find another man who could make her feel the way Jake made her feel?

The expression which came into the blue eyes was difficult to decipher. 'You'd better take that bath,' he said, 'before we have everybody else down here.'

Karen bit her lip as he turned back to the stela. For a moment there she had been on the verge of revealing something she didn't want to acknowledge, even to herself. Jake had no regard for her beyond the purely physical. There was little point in allowing anything deeper to develop on her side.

CHAPTER EIGHT

NEVER had water felt as good. Immersed in it up to her neck, Karen luxuriated for a few minutes of sheer bliss before using the cake of special 'green' soap to form a minor but effective lather.

Jake was still studying the stela when she emerged. He had a notebook out and appeared to be deciphering the glyphs when, dried and clad in clean clothing, she joined him.

'All through,' she announced. 'If you're staying here I'll go and let the others know about the place.'

'I'll come back with you,' he said, returning the notebook to his shirt pocket. 'I need a change of clothing myself.'

The sun was way down. It was going to be dark in less than an hour, Karen reckoned. The heat had diminished to a degree which, while not exactly comfortable, was at least bearable. This and the very early morning were the times of day she liked best. She felt both physically and mentally renewed after her bath.

They went in single file, with Jake in the lead. Just short of the camp-site, he motioned her to stop, taking her by the arm to point her in the direction he was looking. At first she could see nothing in the leafy green foliage of the tree, then gradually she discerned the shape of some large animal, hanging upside-down and motionless from a branch.

'Sloth,' he said. 'They're not often seen.'

'They're normally nocturnal, aren't they?' she queried, drawing a quick glance and lift of the dark brows.

'Right. What else do you know?'

'Only that they almost never come down to the ground because they can only crawl, and that they're capable of inflicting a nasty wound with their claws if attacked. No big deal.'

'You're better informed than most, all the same.'

He made no attempt to release his grasp on her arm. Light as it was, she could feel the imprint of each and every finger burning into her skin. The side of her breast brushed the back of his fingers as he turned her square on to him, causing her to draw in a sudden sharp breath, swiftly smothered by the pressure of his lips on hers.

The kiss left her yearning. Standing there, she longed to throw her arms about his neck and draw the proud head back down to her.

'There's a whole lot more to you than I first envisaged,' he said. 'I know no other woman capable of taking what you've taken these past few days and still coming up smiling.' He slid a finger down the line of her cheek and along her jawbone, tracing the firm structure beneath the skin. 'No other woman,' he repeated softly.

Heart hammering, pulses racing, she gazed at him with darkened eyes. Shorn of the sardonicism she had come to expect from him, he was irresistible.

He was that anyway, came the wry rider. There was no future in it, of course. Once this was over, he would go his way and she would go hers. Right now that wasn't her main concern. What was important was keeping him from guessing the extent of her developing feelings for him.

'Hardly an original line,' she scoffed with deliberation.

Just for a moment the lean features seemed to stiffen, then he laughed and let her go. 'You're right at that. I'll need to take more care.'

Their return to the camp-site together did not go unnoted. It was obvious, from the expression on Mike's face, what he for one was thinking. The fact that he was more than half right didn't help.

'I found a pool deep enough for bathing,' Karen announced, somewhat unnecessarily, considering her damp hair. 'It's all yours now.'

'There's a stela buried in the grass,' Jake told Roger. 'Worth recording, while the light lasts. The bath can come after.'

The sun was on the verge of setting by the time they had finished filming. Karen went back to camp, leaving the men to strip off for their plunge into the pool. She could hear the sound of their voices through the intervening trees, the hearty male laughter over some no doubt ribald comment. As odd man out, so to speak, she envied them that camaraderie.

Santino and Juan had stayed behind to finish setting up. Neither of them spoke any English, and Karen had long given up on attempts to talk to them in their own language. She hung up the clothing she had rinsed through, and sorted out her pack, listening with an ear grown accustomed to the sounds of the jungle about her.

Spitted over the fire, the wild turkeys Luz had shot earlier were beginning to release savoury aromas that caused the mouth to water in anticipation. Food hadn't been any problem so far. In addition to the fish and turkey, they had found papaya and plantains in abundance.

Forty-eight hours from now, providing nothing untoward happened, they should have reached their destination. Another couple of days after that should see them on their way back. Whether Roger would decide to go on to Tikal before returning to Guatemala City was still open to question. He might well consider that they had enough material to go with.

The likelihood of her seeing Jake in person again once they were back in England was remote, unless he himself initiated a meeting. There was no guarantee of that, Karen acknowledged. Where Jake Rothman was concerned there was no guarantee of anything. Out of sight, she would probably soon be out of mind too.

Eaten with the fingers, the turkey proved as good as it smelled. Sipping freshly brewed coffee from a plastic mug afterwards, Karen knew a sense of contentment that even the mosquitoes couldn't dispel. The hustle and bustle of city life was going to seem strange after this. At the moment she had no wish at all to get back to it.

Jake and Roger were deep in discussion. With little chance of having him catch her at it, Karen allowed herself the luxury of watching the former as he talked— remembering the immeasurable pleasure of his lips on her body. 'Having had you once, I'm going to want you again,' he had said. Well, she felt the same way. The difference being that for her it went far beyond simple lust. Against every instinct, against all reason, she was in love with the man. No use hiding from it any longer. Not that the admittance was any comfort.

Lounging close by, Mike was doing his own watching. 'You're fooling yourself if you think anything is going to come of it,' he said, low-toned, startling her because she had forgotten his presence. 'He's just using you. The way we'd all like to, given half a chance!'

Karen forced herself to turn her head and meet the jeering gaze. 'I wondered how long it would take for you to show yourself in your true colours,' she said with control. 'Don't class everyone the same.'

His laugh was harsh. 'We're all men, sweetheart. What would you expect? You're no holy innocent yourself, so don't try coming the high and mighty. I know what's going on between you and Rothman. I saw the two of you down by the river last night.'

Karen stared at him in sick dismay, too stunned for prevarication. 'You were . . . there?'

'I saw him go after you, so I waited a few minutes then followed him. You were both too engrossed by then to hear anything, but I saw plenty.' The smile was slow and suggestive. 'A real little raver when you get going, aren't you?'

'You . . . Peeping Tom!' It sounded ridiculous even as she said it, but she could think of nothing more adequate at the moment. Common sense told her he could have actually seen very little, considering the lack of light, but that in no way reduced the degradation. She added starkly, 'You're not a man, Mike, you're a worm!'

His eyes glittered in the firelight. 'I'll show you how much of a man I am before we're through with this trip! Why should Rothman have it all? Share and share alike, that's my motto!'

She should ignore him, Karen knew, but the insult cut too deep. 'Not where I'm concerned,' she hissed. 'I wouldn't have you near me for a pension!'

She got up and went to start erecting her mosquito net. They would all be turning in soon, so it wouldn't seem too strange if she chose to go now. She needed to be on her own for a while.

Lying there listening to the men talking, she felt a total misfit. Jake had been right from the first: she shouldn't have come. Mike couldn't be blamed too much for considering her an easy conquest, although nothing could excuse his behaviour. From here on in she had to steer clear of any further entanglement with Jake. Like Roger, she would concentrate on the job alone.

They reached their destination around noon of the third day. Smaller than the lower lake, this one was partially covered in a thick growth of water cabbage. The wall of greenery at which Luz began confidently hacking looked impenetrable, but, once through the outer layer, it became possible to move more freely.

The ruins they were seeking lay some short distance into the forest. Gazing at the semi-exposed stonework, Karen could imagine the thrill Luz must have experienced on first stumbling on the site. Luz explored for exploration's sake, Jake had told her once when she'd asked. Like Humboldt's and Bonpland's, his life was devoted to that purpose, with the occasional job such as this one for maintenance.

Santino and Juan set to with a will to clear a space to make camp. They used the lethal-looking machetes like extensions of their arms, slashing away with apparent disregard for life and limb, yet never once missing their aim.

Karen found a seat on a piece of broken stone, heart jerking when Jake came to join her.

'You've been avoiding me,' he stated. 'Any particular reason?'

'I'd have thought the reason was obvious,' she said.

He studied her profile, eyes narrowed against the light slanting through the trees. 'Rather a sudden change of mind, wasn't it?'

'Not really.' She was determined not to give way. 'It should never have happened in the first place.'

'Too true, but it did, and there's no getting away from the fact that we both wanted it,' he returned inexorably. 'Or are you trying to deny that too?'

Karen drew in a shaky breath. 'Why don't you just leave me alone?'

There was a pause before he answered. When he did it was on a suddenly rueful note. 'Because I can't. I knew from the first that I wouldn't be able to stay clear. That's the main reason I didn't want you along. You don't follow any of the accepted patterns.'

'Accepted by whom? Men?' Her laugh sounded brittle. 'There are plenty of others around just as ready as I am to go out on a limb for what they want.'

'I'm not talking about hard-headed female ambition,' he said. 'I've seen plenty of that, believe me! You're something else.'

He had made no attempt to touch her, yet she could feel the hairs on her arms prickling as if from direct contact with the sun-stoked heat of his body. The hunger inside her had nothing to do with lack of food.

She said huskily, 'So...what?'

'So I'd like to continue the relationship after we get back.'

Karen made herself look into the steady blue eyes, trying, without success, to read the mind behind them. 'To what purpose?' she asked.

The shrug was brief. 'Remains to be seen.'

'I was under the impression,' she said slowly, 'that you were heavily involved with Elena Sleeman.'

His expression scarcely altered. 'What gave you that idea?'

'I suppose she did,' Karen admitted. 'It was obvious at the party that she looked on you as her property.'

Jake smiled faintly. 'Elena's a woman accustomed to having men at her feet. She regards us all as her property.'

'Then you're saying there's nothing between you?'

'Nothing that affects us. I already told you I was no saint. I'm no monk either. I'm thirty-four years old, and normally adjusted—as you might have gathered already. That doesn't mean I'm indiscriminate.' His tone deepened. 'I want to make love to you again, Karen. If I have to wait much longer I'm going to blow a fuse!'

It crossed her mind then that this whole conversation might have been aimed towards that very purpose—a thought she swiftly dismissed because it wasn't what she wanted to believe. If she loved this man she had to learn to trust him. In any case, she could hardly wait to be with him again herself.

He read her answer in her eyes, his smile slow and expressive. 'Just one thing,' he added. 'You put Roger in the picture as of now.'

'I already have,' she said. 'Two days ago, in fact.'

'Good.' He paused, gaze seeking the subject under discussion. 'How did he take it?'

'The way he takes everything—equably.' She tagged on swiftly, 'I honestly didn't realise how he felt, Jake. And it certainly had nothing to do with his marriage breaking up. I just wish things could work out for him, that's all.'

'You plan on staying with him job-wise?'

'Yes.'

His glance came back to her. 'He asked you to stay on?'

'Yes,' she said again. 'He sees no reason why the two things can't be separated.'

'He's talking through his hat,' came the blunt response. 'You'd do better looking for another job once we're home.'

'I'll think about it,' Karen promised. At the moment she would have promised him anything. She resolved to look no further than the here and now—to take each and every day as it came. Just to know that Jake felt something for her was enough to be going on with.

They spent the rest of the daylight hours filming. Jake wielded a machete alongside Luz and the Indians with a skill that bespoke previous experience. From time to time he would pause to examine the emerging stonework, with a commentary for the benefit of the viewers to come.

The small area they were tackling contained the substantial remains of a square-topped tower with a steep flight of steps carved into its tapering face. It was this, rising from the surrounding jungle, that Luz had first seen. Green with verdigris, and covered in clinging vines, it stood at the end of what appeared to have been an avenue lined with stelae.

Probably a ceremonial centre, Jake announced. A place of worship to the gods. With the time and facilities available, it was obviously going to be impossible to uncover more than a fraction of the site. Any artefacts that might come to light would remain the property of the Guatemalan government, but only if they found indications that the place had been of some particular importance would their discovery be turned over to an excavation team.

'Another full day should give us enough material for our purpose,' declared Jake over supper. 'Hopefully, that stone hammer-head Luz found won't be the only artefact we come up with. The viewers will expect a whole lot more.'

'We should have brought a few things with us and salted the place,' put in Mike. 'Who would have known?'

Jake didn't even bother to glance the other man's way. 'We would. We'll be starting work as soon as the light's good enough, and resting up during the hottest part of the day.' Just for a moment his eyes sought Karen's, although his expression didn't alter. 'No point in rushing things.'

'I'm planning on taking in Tikal before we go back,' said Roger a little abruptly. 'I appreciate what you said earlier about its having been seen so often on travelogues, but we can use it to give some idea of how this place would have looked in its heyday. We can fly directly back to Guatemala City from there.'

'You're calling the shots,' Jake agreed. 'I was only thinking of the time element.' He stretched and yawned. 'I don't know about anybody else, but I'm for turning in. Tomorrow's going to be a long, hard day.'

Tonight was going to seem even longer, reflected Karen wryly. If only the two of them could find somewhere to be alone together. There was so much she had to learn about him, so much she wanted to know. All very well to talk about seeing each other after they got back home, but that was ages away.

The howler monkeys had quietened as usual with the onset of darkness. The eerie, almost human scream which rang out of the darkness of the jungle set them going again with renewed vigour.

'Jaguar kill,' said Luz succinctly.

'Is it likely to come near the camp?' asked Nigel on a note which echoed Karen's own feelings.

Luz shook his head, no sign of humour in the dark face. 'Human meat holds little appeal compared to the tender flesh of a monkey or deer. You may sleep easy in your beds tonight.'

It wasn't the thought of prowling cats that kept Karen from sleeping. Gazing up through the filmy muslin, she went over and over everything Jake had said earlier. Had he really meant it, or had he simply been saying it? Was what she felt for him love or simply infatuation? She was no longer sure of the difference.

Tonight he was sleeping right next to her again. The movement as he lifted his net tensed every nerve in her body.

'I'm going down to the lake,' he whispered. 'Give it five minutes, then come after me.'

It took her all of that to decide whether or not to obey the command. It wasn't so much a choice in the end as a necessity. The others appeared to be sleeping soundly— Mike included. Karen slid from the sleeping-bag as silently as she could, and found a torch with which to light her way once she left the circle of firelight.

To either side of the pathway hacked out that day lay a green tidal wave of foliage, already sending out new shoots. Once, the torchlight caught a pair of eyes glowing from the darkness, although, to judge from the sound of its hasty departure, the owner was as disinclined to linger as Karen was herself. So much for the mesmerisation theory, she thought. After so many days of it, the jungle no longer held any major terrors for her. Most things out there were far more nervous of her than she was of them.

Jake was waiting for her on the lake shore. He had lit one of his rare cheroots to help ward off mosquito attack.

'I was beginning to think you weren't coming,' he said.

Karen went into his arms like a homing pigeon. There was no point in hanging back, she figured, when she had declared herself so thoroughly by following him at all. His kiss left little to be desired by way of a declaration on his part.

'I've been driving myself crazy these last few days remembering what it felt like to hold you,' he murmured against her hair. His hands moved possessively over the contours of her body, moulding her closer. 'Now you know what you do to me!'

Karen's laugh was low. 'Only the same as you do to me.'

'Except not as obviously. That's where women have the advantage. No outward signs.' He groaned deep in his throat as she moved sensuously against him. 'And to think I almost stopped you from coming with us!'

'Is this the only reason you're glad I'm here?' she asked.

'No,' he said. 'Although it's all part and parcel.' He held her a little away from him to look into her shadowed face, his own softened from its normal incisive lines. 'You weave a pretty hefty spell.'

'Unintentionally.' She was smiling, bolstered by his mood and manner. 'I really thought you detested me, Jake.'

'Self-defence. I believed you were involved with Roger.'

'Even after I denied it?'

The strong mouth slanted. 'I've been lied to before.'

'It seems to me,' Karen said softly, 'that you've been mixing with the wrong people.'

'You could be right at that.' His voice had roughened. 'I warn you, I'm a possessive character.'

'So am I,' she responded, warmed by the promise of a future together inherent in that statement.

She wanted to tell him then that she loved him, but it was too soon, too emotional, too tying. She reached up instead and drew the dark head down to hers, putting her lips to his with all the pent-up passion of the last few days. He answered in kind, sliding both hands under her T-shirt to caress her bare back with a touch that made her quiver. She had never wanted anything, she thought dazedly, as much as she wanted this man.

It took him bare seconds to rid them both of their scanty clothing. Karen buried her face in the whorls of dark hair covering his chest, tasting the salt on his skin, savouring the emotive male scent of him. He was so strong, so vital, his body tautly muscled without an ounce of surplus flesh. All man, and all hers, came the exultant thought as he bore her to the ground beneath him. As she was his. The two of them together, for all time.

If their lovemaking had been good the first time it was infinitely more so tonight. Jake cherished every inch of her with his lips, kissing each closed eye, gently nibbling the tender lobes of her ears, moving on down the length of her throat to tease each nipple into tingling, aching prominence before continuing his quest over waist and hip and fluttering abdomen to reach the silky cluster and carry her to the very peak of fulfilment.

Only not the highest peak, because that was still to come. To be one with Jake was the ultimate experience. Holding him, feeling him inside her, Karen knew she could want no one else. He was the only man she was ever going to love this way.

The words trembled on her lips, yet something deep down still held them back. Then it was too late because the world was turning over, spinning her out into star-spangled space.

They bathed in the lake before making their way back to camp. Luz was up, tending the fire, when they reached it. Karen would have hung back, but Jake drew her forward, meeting the other man's steady glance with masculine aplomb.

'You go back to bed; I'll stay up for a while,' he said softly. 'See you in the morning.'

There was no movement from any of the other sleeping-bags. Karen could only trust that everyone was as dead to the world as they appeared. She lay awake for what seemed like an age, watching the two men by the fire and wondering what they were talking about. Not her, she was sure. Jake wasn't that kind of man. He was her kind of man, and she loved him—would always love him. Nothing could change that now.

CHAPTER NINE

SHAPED like the claw-armed paw of a jaguar, the sceptre was intact in almost every detail. Karen gazed at it wonderingly, scarcely able to credit that the last person to touch it had been dead for centuries.

Jake had unearthed a small cache of objects from beneath a pile of rubble which had once formed the inner wall of a small and possibly once secret room, each one priceless in its antiquity. In addition to the sceptre there was a ceremonial staff carved from indestructible ironwood, incense jars and clay figurines.

Roger was in some seventh heaven. Had he ordered it, things couldn't have worked out better, he declared. Howard had captured the very moment of discovery on camera; there was no need to re-set the scene.

Most of the clay articles were broken, although it might be possible to piece one or two together again from the shards lying around, Jake believed. He had the sceptre and staff carefully packed for transportation, but left the rest for any future expeditions to deal with. Archaeological exploration was secondary to the job he was here to do. Even though his fingers were obviously itching to continue, he had neither time nor facilities for an extended dig.

'Do you think they'll send in a team?' asked Karen when he reluctantly called it a day. 'I'd love to see the whole site opened up.'

'They might,' he said. 'Then again, they might not. Financing a dig comes expensive.' He rubbed dusty hands down the seat of his trousers, a smile touching his lips as he glanced at her. 'Looking forward to a little civilised living again?'

She smiled back, pulses registering the sheer stimulation of his presence. 'I can't say I've really missed it all that much. There have been compensations.'

Blue eyes took on a darker hue. 'We aim to please.'

Mike was watching the two of them, his mouth set in a sneering line. Karen felt her smile stiffen, and saw Jake's brows draw together as he followed the line of her glance.

She said hurriedly, 'I'd better go and sort out my things ready for leaving in the morning.' There was little to sort, but she couldn't bear to have Mike sully their whole relationship with that knowing look of his.

They ate wild turkey again for supper, along with some of the dried vegetables they had brought with them. From where she sat, Karen could see the squared top of the Maya tower outlined by a stray shaft of moonlight. Sacrifices had been performed up there, along with acts of self-mutilation to propitiate the gods. She shuddered at the thought, thankful that such times were long gone.

'Goose walk over your grave?' asked Howard casually at her side.

'Something like that.' She glanced his way, aware that this was the first conversational overture he had ever cast in her direction. 'I was thinking how fortunate we are to be here now and not then.'

'Good for the priesthood, dodgy for the rest,' he agreed. 'You'd have been sacrificed for sure. They always chose the best-looking maidens.'

'Well, thank you, sire.' She kept her tone as light as his. 'How come you know so much about it?'

'My wife's a mine of information on many a subject,' he said. 'She read up on the Maya when she knew I was coming on this job. Seems they weren't nearly as bad as the Toltecs and Aztecs when it came to bloodletting.'

'So Jake said.' She was aware of the suddenly shrewd glance. Was it possible to give herself away just by mentioning Jake's name? she wondered. She added unhurriedly, 'Does your wife ever object to the amount of time you spend away from home, Howard—or is that too personal a question?'

His shrug was non-committal. 'We get by. You'll be spending a fair amount of time travelling yourself if you stay with Roger.'

'True, but I'm not married.'

'Not yet.' There was a brief pause, a change of tone. 'If you'll take a spot of advice from someone old enough to be your father, keep a wary eye on Mike. He's not used to taking a back seat.'

Karen tried to laugh the moment off. 'I didn't realise he was!'

'You know what I'm talking about. I'll grant you, Rothman's the better bet, only——'

'It isn't like that!' The denial was out before she could stop it. She glanced around, thankful that everyone else seemed otherwise occupied, looking back to the man at her side with reluctance. '*I'm* not like that.'

'I didn't think you were,' he returned levelly. 'Some women play on their sex appeal, others take no account of it. You can't come on a jaunt like this and expect to be regarded as one of the guys. You've got Nigel so as he hardly knows what day it is.' He shook his head as she made to speak. 'He's unlikely to act on it; Mike's something else. He's got a touch of the primitive where his urges are concerned—thinks women are there to serve and satisfy the male of the species. He doesn't usually find any shortage of takers either.'

Karen said slowly, 'You seem to know him well.'

'We've worked together a fair time. He's good at his job, and easy enough to get along with. Providing he's not suffering from deprivation, that is. He's been like a bear with a sore head this last day or two. Jealousy, frustration, call it what you like. Just try to keep the cart on the wheels is all I'm saying.'

It was obviously useless, Karen reflected wryly, to keep on denying any cause for Mike to be jealous. If Howard was aware that she and Jake had something going then so, probably, did the rest. Luz, for instance, had known from the beginning. They would need to be more circumspect in future. No more slipping away for clandestine meetings at night. In less than a week they would be back in San Samoza, then Tikal and home. If Jake was serious about furthering their relationship he would appreciate her feelings.

Not that it was going to be easy for her to forgo physical contact either, if it came to that. Looking at him across the firelit space, she craved to be in his arms again right now.

As if sensing her regard, he glanced her way. With Howard observing, she found it difficult to act naturally, shifting her gaze back to the latter with a bright smile and some contrived remark regarding the day's filming.

If Howard realised why she was suddenly so interested in camera angles it made no difference to his answers. He was always prepared to discuss his work. Listening to him, Karen tried to put everything else to the back of her mind. She would talk to Jake later, if the chance arose, and make him understand.

The rain came at around ten o'clock and went on for an hour or more. Not for the first time, they all blessed the corozo fronds from which the *champas* were constructed. The tough texture was impervious to the heaviest rain.

Far from cooling the atmosphere, the dampness served only to increase the humidity. Sleep didn't come easily to anyone that night. Tossing and turning within her steaming cocoon, Karen could only think longingly of cool showers and iced drinks. Never again, she vowed, would she take such things for granted.

They struck camp early, although not before Howard had got some superb footage of the partially exposed Mayan remains wreathed in early-morning mist. Karen was torn between relief to be on the way home, and regret that it hadn't been possible to delve further into the ancient mystery of the vanished race. She could appreciate Jake's feelings as they turned their backs on the sight for the last time.

Even with the sceptre and staff for evidence, it was doubtful, he had said, that any organised dig would be arranged in the near future. Having existed for centuries, the remains weren't going to disappear altogether in a few months or even years, and it was doubtful whether anyone else would stumble on it the way Luz had done.

Karen wanted to ask what he planned on doing after this job was wrapped up, but with others present she knew she would find it difficult to sound as casual as she would have liked. His suggestion that they continue to see each other after their return to England meant little if he wasn't going to be there very long.

It was probably imagination on her part, she assured herself, that his attitude towards her this morning appeared somewhat cool. Either that, or he was simply offsetting any impression the rest might have gained of a burgeoning interest. She hadn't told him about Mike's midnight spying, and didn't intend doing so. It was bad enough for her to know.

The younger man's attitude was more easily defined. When he spoke to her at all it was with a scarcely concealed contempt that she did her best to ignore. That his demeanour had not gone unnoted by others in the party, however, was brought home to her that evening when Roger drew her aside on the pretext of discussing some aspect of the day's work.

'Has Mike been bothering you?' he asked bluntly.

'In what way?' Karen prevaricated, eliciting a faint smile.

'How many ways are there? Judging from the way he's been acting this last day or two, he's suffering from a badly bent ego. If I had to make a guess I'd say he tried something on with you and got turned down. Close?'

'He hasn't touched me,' she declared truthfully. 'If he's suffering from anything at all it's probably the heat—the way we all are.'

'Some more than others. You always look good.' He held up a hand in mute apology as her expression altered. 'Just an observation. I gave up hope once I realised how you felt about Jake.'

Karen said huskily, 'Do I make it so obvious?'

'Maybe not to the others. I'm sensitised.' He hesitated before going on, 'Try not to take this as sour grapes, but I rather think he's spoken for already.'

'By Elena Sleeman?' She tried to keep her voice level.

'Well, yes.' Roger sounded surprised. 'Did Jake tell you himself, or is it just a guess?'

'It isn't true.' She couldn't stop herself from saying it. 'There's nothing serious between them.'

'Elena doesn't seem to share that view. She told me they were to be married quite soon.'

'I don't believe it.' Karen spoke with an emphasis designed to cover the sudden heaviness creeping into her heart. 'Jake wouldn't...' She broke off, the tell-tale warmth rising under skin at the look in Roger's eyes. 'He wouldn't lie,' she said dully.

'You mean he flatly denied it?'

'Well, not in so many words, I suppose.' Karen cast her mind back, trying to recall exactly what Jake *had* said about his relationship with the beautiful Guatemalan. The conversation came back to her with sickening clarity. 'Nothing that affects us,' he had returned when she'd asked him if there was anything between them. She had taken that to mean that anything there had been was over, on his part, at least. But if Elena genuinely believed they were to be married...

'Sorry if it's come as a shock,' proffered Roger on a wry note. 'I wouldn't have had Jake Rothman down for that kind of louse either, although he can be pretty ruthless at times. I realised early on that he was attracted to you, of course. I guess that's why he was so adamantly against having you along. All the same, he had no right to...' It was his turn to break off in mid-sentence, mouth taking on a rueful cast. 'Just as I've no right to be preaching. I just wanted to be sure you knew how things were, Karen. I'd hate to see you badly hurt.'

Too late, she thought hollowly. Her whole world had turned upside-down. Jake had simply been making time with her; he didn't really care. Well, two could play that game, although it was going to call for every ounce of acting ability she possessed to convince him that her interest was equally shallow.

Opportunity arose over supper in the shape of Nigel Morris. A part of Karen's mind shrank from using him in such a way, but her need was stronger than the pangs of conscience. Seating herself beside him, she drew him out to talk about himself, listening with flattering attention as he expounded on the subject. Even without glancing once in his direction, she could feel Jake's gaze from time to time. Her senses were tuned to the waves emanating from him, though not quite finely enough to be totally sure of his reactions. Whatever he was feeling, it was a positive emotion. That much she *could* be sure of.

The night stayed dry inasmuch as it didn't rain, but the humidity was ever-present. Awakening at first light to the howling, grown almost common-place, Karen plucked damp cotton away from her skin and knew she wouldn't sleep again. The river was scarcely deep enough at this point for full submersion, but more than enough for washing. If she went now she could be through before any of the others woke up.

The thought was all it took to get her moving. Luz and Santino were showing signs of life as she left the camp. By the time she got back coffee would be made and breakfast waiting. They had all become accustomed to making do with whatever had been left from the previous night, supplemented where necessary by supplies from their stock. As diets went, Karen had known worse. She had once spent a whole week in the Scottish Highlands, living off the land, with far less satisfying results.

The undergrowth was sparse enough to allow reasonably free passage through to the riverbank from the spot where Luz had chosen to set up camp. With the light steadily growing, she found little difficulty in reaching her goal.

She discarded the cotton pyjamas to step knee-deep into the slow-moving water and scoop handfuls of it over herself, relishing the delicious feel of the liquid splashing down her back. Even the sight of a long and sinuous snake gliding over the surface some distance away couldn't detract from the pleasure too much. She simply kept a weather-eye on the creature until it slid from sight into the brush bordering the far bank.

It was only then, as she shifted her gaze a fraction, that she saw the deer. About to drink, the small red-coated animal either saw or scented her at the same time, and froze. The low snarling growl from the undergrowth had the same effect on Karen. She stood as if turned to stone as the big spotted cat exploded from its cover to flatten the defenceless creature to the ground.

Crouching over its kill, ears laid back and tail rigid, the jaguar glared with burning eyes across the river to where Karen stood rooted. It could be on her in seconds, the tiny part of her mind still working on a rational level warned, even as her instincts told her to turn and run.

'Stay perfectly still,' said Jake very softly from somewhere to her rear. 'Let him see you're not threatening his claim.'

Anything less threatening Karen found difficult to imagine. From locked rigidity, her knees turned to pure jelly when the animal finally picked up the limp deer by the scruff of the neck and melted back into the jungle. For a long time afterwards, she knew, she would see a vivid picture of that magnificent head every time she closed her eyes. The image was burned into her retina.

'You can come on out now,' Jake advised. 'In fact, right now!'

Karen turned nervelessly to obey, scarcely aware of her nudity as she moved through water that felt suddenly more like treacle to join him. Face grim, he wrapped the towel he held ready around her. Only then did reaction begin to set in. Trembling uncontrollably, she looked up at him with eyes wide and dark in a face drained of colour.

'I thought it was going to attack,' she whispered shakily.

'If you'd moved or called out it might have,' he said. 'Not for food, but in defence of its kill. You're one of the few people to see a jaguar in such close-up in its natural habitat—the *only* one I know of to actually witness a kill. I arrived a fraction too late.'

He was talking for the sake of it, Karen thought: giving her time to recover from the shock. She was recovering too. Enough so to realise that his mood was far from solicitous. The blue eyes were like ice.

'Why don't you say it?' she asked resignedly. 'I shouldn't be here on my own.'

'You shouldn't be here, period,' came the clipped retort. 'I was right about that, at least.'

Her head came up, pride reasserting itself at the memory of what she had learned from Roger about this man whom she had so foolishly believed she loved. 'But wrong about everything else?'

'So it appears.' There was no softening of tone. 'It's all a game to you, isn't it? An expert player, I'll grant you. That blow hot, blow cold, can't help myself routine of yours was a sure-fire winner where I was concerned.'

She said stonily, 'I don't know what you're talking about.'

'Don't give me that! You've had Mike dangling on a string for months.'

'He told you that?'

'Are you denying it?'

Her chin jutted at his tone. 'I can't speak for Mike's feelings, only for my own actions.'

'If you gave him the same personal attention you've been giving Howard and Nigel lately he had some reason to take it as a come-on. And who's next on the list? Luz? You might find him a tougher proposition.'

Her face flamed. 'If you're suggesting what I think you are you've no right!'

'Oh, I'm not saying you offer everyone the same kind of favours you've extended to me,' came the derisive response. 'I'm prepared to accept that you found yourself out of your depth for once—even if only as a sop to my own ego. What I'm not prepared to do is stand by and let you give Nigel, for one, any false ideas in the process of taking me down a peg or two. Don't bother denying that either,' he added as she opened her mouth to speak. 'I'm not fool enough to fall for the wide-eyed prot-estations bit again.'

Karen's voice sounded hollow in her ears. 'Why would I need to take you down a peg or two?'

The shrug was brief. 'Part of the process. Except that your judgement was faulty this time. I'm not down— I'm out.'

It was all over between them—that was what he was saying. Counter accusations trembled on her lips, held back by the desperate need not to let him see how deeply she was hit. Eyes as cold as his, she said, 'It was nice while it lasted.'

Some fleeting and unreadable expression passed across the tanned face, then it hardened again into the same unremitting mask. 'I think we owe each other a little fonder goodbye than that.'

Pulled up hard against him, with his mouth bruising hers, Karen could feel the towel slipping and knew that it would fall away the moment he released her. Derogatory though the kiss was meant to be, it elicited a helpless response. Physically, he was still the same man; her body refused to recognise the lessons learned. She had to fight to retain some emotional control.

The cough came from only a few yards away. Jake put her unhurriedly from him, giving her the opportunity to grab the sliding towel before it went too far as he turned to face the newcomer.

Luz looked impassive as always. 'We have a problem,' he announced. 'Nigel is sick.'

Jake wasted no time on enquiries. If Luz had come to fetch him it had to be serious. 'Get dressed and back to camp,' he clipped to Karen without looking her way.

Having made her own way here, she was obviously capable of making her own way back, she thought numbly as the two men disappeared among the trees. Right now she had more to concern her than the wildlife in the area. Even her heartache paled into temporary insignificance beside news of Nigel's condition. Any illness out here was bad. Medical supplies were limited to the basics.

Mike was the only one to note her arrival in their midst. The others were all too concerned with the sweating, groaning figure around which they were grouped. Nigel looked like death. From the manner in which he was clutching his stomach, the pain had to be intense.

Kneeling at his side, Jake looked for once at a total loss. 'Coming on this fast, it could be appendix, I suppose,' he declared without any real conviction.

'The pain is too high up for that.' Karen had said it before she was aware of formulating any opinion. She met the blue gaze without a flicker. 'It could be simple gastritis, caused by eating something that disagreed with him.'

Dark brows lifted sardonically. 'You've had medical training?'

'I'm an accredited first-aider,' she returned, refusing to be put either down or out by the sarcasm. She sank to her knees on Nigel's other side, smiling reassurance as she gently probed the area around the lower right half of his abdomen. 'Do you feel anything there?'

Somebody snorted in the background. Probably Mike, Karen thought. He was the only one likely to be reading double meanings at a time like this. In too much discomfort to care, Nigel shook his head. 'Higher,' he gasped. 'Cramps.' He doubled over as another spasm gripped him, drawing his knees up towards his chest in an effort to ease the pain, and retching drily.

He had vomited already, Karen noted, which meant that if the attack was food orientated at least the residue was gone. On the other hand, it could be a viral infection. She closed her eyes while she tried to recall what treatment, if any, could be applied, opening them again to find Jake studying her with narrowed eyes.

'So?' he prompted.

'There isn't a great deal we can do except wait for the inflammation to subside,' she said with a confidence she was far from feeling. 'Obviously, he can't be moved before then.'

'How long?' The question was terse.

Karen lifted her shoulders. 'I'm not a doctor. Twenty-four hours, at least. A dose of magnesia should help. There's a bottle in the medical pack.'

She went to find it, coming back to bend and slide an arm behind Nigel's head in support as she put the plastic measure to his lips. 'Afraid I can't do any more,' she said with regret.

With the cramp attack apparently subsiding for the moment, he gave her a look of near-worship. 'Thanks,' he whispered.

Jake got to his feet, but made no effort to offer her a hand. 'Let's give him some air,' he said. 'What there is of it.' To Karen herself he added quietly, 'You sure about this?'

'Not one hundred per cent,' she confessed, turning away so that Nigel couldn't overhear what was being said. 'As I already mentioned, I'm not a doctor. I'm reasonably sure it isn't appendicitis, though.'

His mouth twisted. 'I'll bow to your greater knowledge. If it's something he ate how come we aren't all suffering the same symptoms?'

'Because not everyone is allergic to the same thing,' she returned. 'It could have been that fungi Santino found—or even a sudden susceptibility to turkey meat.'

'She's right.' Luz was standing by. 'I've seen it before. Twenty-four hours with just water to drink and he should be improved. I'll make sure we have a good supply ready sterilised. For now, we have to make the best of things.'

'I'll sit with Nigel,' Karen declared as the other man moved off. 'I can at least keep the flies off him.' She forced herself to look Jake directly in the eye. 'No other motive, I assure you.'

There was no relenting of expression on his part. He looked as hard as nails. 'No point in it any more, is there?'

Karen bit down hard on her lip as she turned away. Telling herself she didn't care was one thing, feeling it something else entirely.

CHAPTER TEN

Roger took advantage of the unexpected halt to do some reviewing after breakfast.

'You've done all you can for him,' he said when Karen showed reluctance to leave the invalid's side. 'I need you.'

'I'm feeling better,' Nigel assured her weakly. 'The nausea's gone, and the cramps aren't as bad. I might be fit to go on by this afternoon.'

'It won't be worth striking camp for a couple of hours,' Karen soothed. 'Far better if we leave it till morning. We're only losing a day. That's not going to upset the schedule to any great degree. Is it?' she appealed to Roger.

'Nothing we can't cope with,' he returned. 'Thank God it was nothing worse than a touch of food poisoning!'

'You're looking a bit drawn yourself,' he added frankly when they were out of earshot of the patient. 'Not coming down with the same thing, I hope?'

Karen shook her head, wondering fleetingly whether it was the time element or her welfare that concerned him the most. 'Just the heat, I expect.'

'It's washing us all out,' he agreed. 'Even Jake, and he's used to it.' He cast her a glance when she failed to respond, and added hesitantly, 'Karen, what I said yesterday—maybe I was mistaken.'

'You weren't mistaken.' Her tone was flat. 'Forget it, Roger.'

'I've half a mind to tell him what I think of him!' he expostulated.

'It isn't that important.' She tried her best to sound convincing. 'The job is. How long do you intend spending at Tikal?'

He accepted the change of subject without demur. 'Depends on how long it takes us to get back to San Samoza from here. We're due back in England by the end of the month, as you already know. With any luck, we'll have a day or two's leeway to rest up before flying out. We'll be using the same place. Jake——' He stopped, mouth wry. 'I didn't mean to bring him up again.'

Karen made no reply for the simple reason that there was nothing she could say. Today was only the twenty-first. Jake was going to be around for some time to come. Not that she would be taking advantage of any leeway. Her return ticket was valid for three months from date of issue. If she could get a flight she would go on ahead of the rest of the unit.

The day passed slowly. Jake joined Luz and Santino on a hunting expedition in the late afternoon, returning with a small deer much like the one Karen had seen killed by the jaguar. No doubt Jake would have told Luz of the cat's proximity, but as it presented little or no danger to their party she supposed there was no great need for caution. She hadn't mentioned it to anyone herself because it might elicit too many awkward questions.

By suppertime, Nigel was well enough to sit up and drink some corozo-nut milk, although obviously very shaky still. Watching him, Karen had serious doubts that he would be fit to travel by morning, but she kept that opinion to herself. They had no facility, and scarcely enough manpower to carry him along with everything else.

With some deliberation she made sure her bed was right next to his that night, disregarding Jake's ironic glance. If the latter wished to read any ulterior motive into the gesture he was at liberty. The hurt he had inflicted hadn't lessened, but it was contained. He would never know how utterly stupid she had been in allowing herself to fall for him, she vowed.

While obviously far from robust, Nigel proclaimed himself almost back to normal next morning. He had slept like a log, he said. Which was more than she had done herself, Karen reflected.

Luz divided the greater part of Nigel's backpack among the rest of them, leaving him with just a few items of lighter equipment to carry. Pale of face, but determinedly game, the latter nibbled on a couple of the nutritious wheaten biscuits from their basic stock while the rest of them finished off the previous night's left-overs.

Toast and marmalade was going to seem a real treat after this, thought Karen. It was odd how the time of day governed the taste-buds.

Able to follow the trail blazed on the inward journey, they made good time. By late afternoon, when they made camp for the night, Nigel was looking almost himself again. He was pathetically grateful for Karen's ministrations, and disinclined to listen to any protests that she had actually been able to do very little.

'You stayed with me,' he said. 'That was a real comfort.' His eyes searched her face with an expression that made her heart sink. 'Karen, after we get back——'

'I'll be looking for another job when we get back,' she interrupted levelly.

His face went blank for a moment, then flushed. 'Not because of me, I hope? I know I must have made it obvious how I feel about you, but . . .'

How was it she could give so many people the wrong impression without even realising it? Karen asked herself painfully as his voice tailed off. Wasn't it possible to be friendly towards a man without having one's motives misread? She had realised early on that Mike was liable to take liberties, and had backpedalled accordingly, but Roger's emotional involvement had come as a complete surprise. And now Nigel. All she needed was to have Howard declare himself and she really would begin to think Jake could be right in his assessment of her!

An assessment Howard shared to a certain extent, she was bound to acknowledge, recalling what he had said a couple of nights ago. It was true that she took no account of her sex appeal because she hadn't been aware of possessing that much.

'It doesn't have anything to do with that,' she said. 'I just don't think this is my kind of thing, that's all.'

'This job's an exception,' Nigel protested. 'The next one won't be anything like. You can't be serious.'

'I'm afraid I am,' she assured him. 'Very.'

He looked totally dispirited. 'Does Roger know?'

Karen shook her head. 'Not yet. And I'd as soon he didn't until after we get back.'

'He's going to be disappointed. I heard him telling Howard you were proving invaluable. You're part of the unit, Karen.'

'Only until we get back home.' She forced a smile. 'Just concentrate on getting better, and forget about it for the time being, will you, please?'

'All right.' He sounded despondent. 'If that's what you want.'

Wanting, she thought unhappily, had nothing to do with it. In future she would make sure to keep herself to herself.

Jake hadn't been near her all day. His approach after supper when she was sorting out her pack ready for morning took her unawares. Not with friendly intent, though, she gathered, quelling the faint hope as she viewed the set features. Now what had she done?

He left her in no doubt with an immediate frontal attack. 'I realise you have to have someone champing at the bit to keep you boosted, but I thought we'd agreed you were to leave Nigel alone?'

There were several retorts Karen could have made; the one she chose to make was far from the wisest. 'We didn't agree, you dictated. I don't take orders from you, Jake.'

'All right, then,' he said with control, 'so I'll put it another way. Either stop encouraging him to think you have a special interest, or I'll tell him about us.'

Karen sat back on her heels to look at him with veiled eyes. He had assumed a squatting position, which brought him down to her level; to anyone watching they would have appeared to be having a casual conversation. His closeness made her ache.

'Tell him what about us?' she enquired with deliberation, and saw a muscle tense in the strong jawline.

'A detailed account, if that's what it takes to turn him off.'

All she had to do was explain that she had already scotched any notions Nigel might have had, but he was making that difficult. She said coolly, 'Why the concern for Nigel, anyway? He's nothing to you.'

'Call it fellow feeling,' he said. 'I know how easy it is to take you at face value.'

'That,' she replied, 'might be applied to us all. Look to your own values before criticising others, Jake!'

Blue eyes narrowed. 'Meaning what exactly?'

Karen took a firm hold on herself. Bringing Elena into it now might suggest a deeper involvement on her part than she had given him to believe. She would rather have him continue to think her as shallow as himself than allow him to even suspect the truth.

Her shrug made light of the statement. 'Meaning you're an unlikely saint. I was hardly your first sexual encounter; I doubt very much that I'll be the last. There's a great difference in degree between that and what you're accusing me of—but, of course, you're male, and a man can't be expected to restrain his natural urges, can he?'

'Not where the lure is irresistible,' came the ironic response. 'You were all of that. I have to admit to missing our sessions. Making love to you was an experience difficult to forget.'

'Don't denigrate the word!' Karen shot at him.

His smile mocked her scorn. 'You'd prefer the cruder expression?'

She swallowed thickly. 'No.'

'Then don't leave yourself open to it. Not that it applies in this instance anyway. We made love, lady. Pure, unadulterated passionate *amour*!'

'Shut up!' Her voice had a tremor. 'I don't want to talk about it.'

'But you still want me,' he said unrelentingly. 'The same way I still want you. A cross we both have to bear.' He pressed himself to his feet in one lithe movement, looking down on her with closed expression. 'I meant what I said. If you need someone to trifle with, why not give Mike another spin? He's unlikely to get hurt.'

And there went another, she thought bitterly as he moved off. The fact that he still wanted her was no solace. For him, it had never gone any deeper than that. She was the fool for allowing herself to care for him—and an even bigger one for still doing so regardless.

With Nigel wholly recovered from his indisposition by the morning, she felt able to avoid any one-to-one contact between them. For his own sake, she told herself, not because of anything Jake had said, although the latter was certainly going to think he was the instigator.

It was partly because of this that she made no attempt to freeze Mike off when he fell back to join her at one point on the trail.

'I guess the romance is over?' he said. 'Bad luck.'

Karen put up a hand to push back the damp hair at her temple, and eased the pack at her back before answering.

'Isn't that what you were aiming for?'

'Me?' He was all innocence. 'How do I come into it?'

'By making out I'd led you on.' She cast him an appraising glance. 'That is what you told Jake, isn't it?'

'I told him the truth,' he said. 'You were all over me until you decided it was Roger's turn for the treatment.'

'That isn't true, and you know it!' she declared with force. 'I never said or did anything to create that impression!'

'You might not have said it, but you sure enough looked it. Those eyes and that body of yours speak volumes to a man.'

'Only those with an over-inflated imagination.'

'No way! You're an out and out tantaliser, Karen. You offer what you've no intention of coming through with.' He paused, voice taking on a new note. 'Apart from

Rothman, that is. I've got to hand it to him. He didn't get short-changed.'

Was there anything to be gained from further appeal? Karen asked herself. Did she really care what Mike thought of her anyway? Perhaps he was right and she did offer some kind of unconscious invitation. Looking from this end, how could she tell?

'I'm sorry you see things that way,' she said. 'There isn't a lot I can do about it.'

'Oh, I wouldn't say that.' His tone was far from casual. 'I've a forgiving nature. You'll need somebody now Rothman's out of the picture.'

Karen gave him a look of pure distaste. 'You really are lower than the low!'

'"All's fair in love and war."'

'Hardly applicable in this case.'

'I wouldn't say that either.' If there had been any banter in him at all it was gone now; he looked and sounded deadly serious. 'I'm crazy about you, Karen. You're driving me round the twist! Just give me a chance, that's all I'm asking.'

Four men, each with a different approach, yet all ultimately after the same thing, she thought with bitter irony. Not one of them had said 'I love you, Karen'. Being a *femme fatale*, albeit an unknowing one, was no spirit-lifter. She had never felt worse.

'There's nothing you could offer me that I'd be interested in,' she said shortly. 'Just leave me alone, Mike. That's all *I* ask!'

Luz was calling a halt for rest and recuperation. Avoiding so much as a glance in Jake's direction, Karen went to join Howard, who was examining his camera.

'Problems?' she asked.

'Nothing I can't fix,' he acknowledged. He added, 'You're looking a bit peaky. Not coming down with the same thing Nigel's had, are you?'

'No,' she said. 'We none of us look too sparkling, if it comes to that. I suppose eight days in the jungle would tax anyone.'

'Especially a lone woman beset by lecherous males,' came the half humorous response. 'Having trouble with Mike again?'

Karen forced a smile. 'Nothing I can't handle.'

'Don't count on it. Eight days without a woman must be something of a record where he's concerned. How he's survived this long without picking up something nasty, the Lord only knows! What I'm saying is, he's suffering the pangs far more than the rest of us, and likely to ignore the consequences if the chance comes his way to relieve the pressure.'

She said blankly, 'You're not suggesting he'd actually...'

'Try rape if all else failed?' Howard supplied as her voice trailed away. 'I wouldn't rule it out. It would be a case of your word against his.'

'And who's likely to believe an out and out Jezebel like me, you mean?'

'Not a description I'd have chosen myself, but you get the general idea. Some men genuinely believe a woman means yes when she says no—or, at the very least, maybe.'

'But you're not one of them?'

He grinned fleetingly. 'If I ever was my wife soon scotched the idea. She could teach you a thing or two about handling men. What Hilary says goes.'

'I'm sure.' Karen smiled back, taking him no more seriously than he meant to be taken. 'I wouldn't mind meeting her some time.'

'It could be arranged.' He looked round as Roger joined them. 'Got something in mind?'

'Luz found some jaguar tracks on the riverbank. Jake wants to make camp here and try to get the animal on camera. It seems they're rare enough now to make it a real scoop if we succeed. Worth the time.'

Not to her, thought Karen wryly as the two men began discussing technicalities. She was desperate for this journey to end. It seemed unlikely that the jaguar would be the same one she had seen the other morning, yet if they were so rare it was also unlikely that there would be two of the creatures within such a relatively small area. Travel through the jungle was much slower for humans than it would be for the animal element. It might even be following them. Curiosity didn't have to be confined to the domestic species of cat.

At Jake's suggestion, a platform was built in one of the larger trees overlooking the stretch of river bank where the footprints had been seen. Disguised by the judicious placing of leafy branches, the hide could not be spotted at all from ground-level.

'Providing the wind stays in the same quarter, we should be OK,' Jake declared back in the camp already made. 'Assuming the animal is still in the area, that is. We'll get ourselves settled before sunset on the chance that it will come back to drink at the same spot before going on the hunt.'

'You're planning on spending the night up there if the cat doesn't show early on?' asked Roger.

'That's right. Dawn would be another optimum time.' Jake paused. 'There's only room for two. Sound will have to be added later if the audio doesn't pick up.'

'No problem,' Mike assured him. 'I've a whole stock to draw on.'

Where his job was concerned, Mike was a different person, Karen reflected, listening to him talk. A pity he had to spoil the image in other directions. Even so, she couldn't really believe he was capable of acting the way Howard had suggested.

She was on the verge of reversing that opinion later on emerging from the brush, which provided the only privacy, to find him lying in wait for her. The fact that the others were within easy calling distance made little immediate impression.

His first words were totally disconcerting. 'I want to apologise,' he said softly. 'I've acted like a pig these last few days. Let's kiss and make up.'

Her breath came out on a long-drawn-out sigh. Not so much a change of heart as of tactic, and hardly subtle at that.

'I'm willing to make up,' she said, 'but the kissing's out.'

'It wouldn't hurt you to make a gesture.' His voice had roughened again. 'I could give you just as good a time as Rothman—maybe better. You must be missing it as much as I am.'

'I'm missing nothing,' she retorted. 'Just get it through your head that I'm not interested, will you, Mike? Now get out of my way!'

'Not without what I came for,' he gritted.

'Leave her alone!' The injunction came from close by, jerking both their heads around in unison. A figure detached itself from the shadowing trees to take a single step forward.

It was Nigel, Karen realised: but a very different Nigel from the quiet, unassuming character they all knew. The moonlight caught the angry glitter in his eyes and revealed a face set in lines of grim determination.

'It's all right,' she assured him. 'No harm done.'

'No, it isn't all right!' Mike had turned to face the younger man, hands clenching into fists at his sides. 'What the hell does it have to do with you?'

'Everything, when it comes to dealing with garbage,' came the contemptuous response. 'You're all of that, you——'

He got no further because Mike launched himself at him, bearing his slighter figure to the ground under an onslaught of blows. Karen yelled at him to stop, and drew a sudden ear-splitting burst of sound from the surrounding jungle as the howler monkeys came awake high in their leafy canopy. The two men rolling on the ground seemed oblivious to the din. Nigel was giving a good account of himself, although obviously getting the worst of it.

Luz was first on the scene, with Santino and Juan close on his heels. The former wasted no time on enquiries but gave the two Indians a signal to grab hold of Mike, while he himself seized hold of Nigel. Roger got there as the two were hauled to their feet, both of them still eager for the fray.

'What the devil is going on?' he demanded above the racket still being raised by the howlers.

'Ask her!' Mike exclaimed with a savage jerk of his head in Karen's direction. 'She caused it!'

'That's not true!' denied Nigel heatedly. 'You were going for her like some randy tom-cat!'

'Stop it, both of you!' Karen was almost at the end of her tether. Trembling, and doing her best to control it, she met Roger's questioning gaze. 'Whatever caused it, it's over now. Can't we leave it at that?'

Jake and Howard's appearance put a halt on whatever reply he might have been about to make to the plea. Jake took in the situation at a glance, and reached an immediate and jaw-steeling conclusion.

'What we might have anticipated,' he clipped. 'I hope you're satisfied.' The last to Karen in a tone that restored her to full fighting spirit.

'It wasn't Karen's fault,' Nigel protested. 'Don't blame her because this louse got fresh!'

Coming on top of 'randy tom cat', the naïve expression brought an involuntary quiver to Karen's lips. She saw Jake's eyes narrow as he glanced at her, and knew he had misread that too. The howlers were quietening down again, the forest settling back to its normal night-time level of sound. Standing there, she felt at odds with everyone and everything.

'Just drop it,' she said with force. 'I'm sick of the whole lot of you!'

It was Jake who answered, voice hard. 'Unfortunately, you're as stuck with us as we are with you.'

'Not necessarily.' She stalked past them all with head held high, ignoring Roger's feeble attempt to detain her. The circle of flickering light cast by the camp fire less than fifty yards away was a beacon impossible to miss. Reaching the clearing, she headed for her bed space to start cramming things haphazardly into her pack.

She sensed rather than heard movement behind her, but she didn't turn.

'What exactly did you have in mind?' asked Jake expressionlessly.

'I'd have thought it obvious,' she flung at him over a shoulder. 'He travels fastest who travels alone!'

'Don't be ridiculous,' he said. 'You're not going anywhere.'

'Try and stop me!'

'Common sense should be enough to stop you. That's assuming you ever had any to start with!' He bent and seized her by the arm when she failed to respond, dragging her up and round. His fingers were like steel bands, his eyes glittering with scarcely controlled anger in the reflected light from the fire. 'Cut it out, will you?'

The others in the party were apparently leaving him to it. Nigel was the only one even looking this way, Karen noted fleetingly.

'Let go of me!' she ground out through clenched teeth. 'You already made your opinion clear enough! Why should you care *what* I do?'

'How I feel has damn-all to do with it,' he jerked back. 'How far do you think you'd get on your own, you little fool?'

He was right, of course, but she had no intention of admitting it. 'I'd as soon risk stepping on a bushmaster as put up with you and the rest of your ilk any longer,' she declared bitterly.

'I was under the impression that Nigel was defending you.'

'I didn't ask for that either. I didn't ask for any of this, no matter what you think!'

Fingers still bruising, he regarded her for a long hard moment. 'The evidence is against you.'

'The way you interpret it, you mean. What do you have to go on? Mike's word? That's worth no more than yours!'

His brows drew together. 'When did I lie to you?'

Too late for retraction, Karen acknowledged. In any case, it was high time he realised that she knew him for what he was.

'Not in so many words, I'll grant you. You're too sharp for that. I wonder if Elena realises how far from faithful her second husband might prove to be!'

It was difficult to read anything from Jake's expression. 'Where did that notion come from?'

'You could say straight from the horse's mouth,' she retorted, 'except that one could hardly apply that description to Elena.'

'*She* told you?'

'She told Roger. The night of the barbecue.'

'He could have misunderstood her.'

Karen shook her head. 'No chance. Why don't you admit it?' She sought for some way to pierce the armour. 'Unless you're afraid of what might be thought.'

'Meaning what?' He was still giving nothing away.

'Meaning that it might make a lot of people believe the rumours were true.'

'And what rumours are we talking about?'

She had gone too far to stop now; she didn't, Karen told herself, want to stop. 'There are those who consider the two of you had an arrangement prior to her marriage. She finished up a very rich woman, didn't she?'

Jake's harsh laugh drew attention from across the fire. 'You think I might have arranged to have the man bumped off too?'

The reply was right there on the tip of her tongue; she bit it back with an effort. Whatever Jake might or might not be, a killer he wasn't. Looking at him, she felt the enmity drain from her, leaving her flat and empty. It was his life, his future. She had never been more than a passing fancy.

She said tonelessly, 'It's none of it important anyway. Not to me.'

For a moment he seemed about to question that statement, then he shrugged and let go of her. 'Just so long as we know where we stand. Let's have no more nonsense about taking off on your own.'

The gesture had been no more than that to start with, Karen acknowledged numbly as he turned away from her to go and join the others. She had known she wouldn't be allowed to simply walk out.

At least she was sure of one thing: Jake hadn't denied that he was to marry Elena, because he couldn't—not without making out the woman was a liar herself. When? was the only question left unanswered.

CHAPTER ELEVEN

THE two men returned to the hide well before dawn. Sleepless herself, Karen was relieved when it started to get light at last.

Dressed, she sat watching Santino make coffee on the replenished fire. Roger joined her there.

'Sorry about last night,' he proffered. 'Seems we're all of us a bit strung up. I had a word with Mike.'

'With what results?' she asked, and saw his shoulders lift.

'He says you asked for it.'

'Do *you* think I did?'

'Of course not.' He hesitated, slanting a swift glance. 'Not intentionally, at any rate. I suppose the circumstances make it difficult for you to keep a low profile. My fault for bringing you along in the first place. I should have known better.'

'You changed your mind,' Karen pointed out. 'I was the one who forced the issue. Taking that into account, Mike might be right. I did ask for it.'

'But not the way he means. You're hardly that type.'

'Thanks.' She hesitated herself before voicing the question, 'Did I really give you the impression I saw you as something more than just my boss, Roger?'

The good-looking features took on a wry cast. 'Probably more a case of wishful thinking. You have a way of making a man feel special—as if he's the only one of interest to you.'

'You mean I flirt?'

'That's not the word. "Concentrate" would be closer. You listen without interrupting—that's rare in a woman, to start with. You make me feel my opinion is of vital importance to you.'

'When it comes to work, it is,' she said. 'I'm eager to learn as much as I possibly can about every aspect of it. If that comes across as something more personal, I'm sorry. I'll try to remember not to be quite so intense about things in future.'

'The way you look doesn't help,' Roger admitted. 'The first time I laid eyes on you, I . . .' He broke off, shaking his head. 'Immaterial now. You turned out to be a good choice whatever. I still don't want to lose you, Karen.'

'I think you have to,' she said carefully. 'The unit will be better for it.'

From his lack of sustained argument, she could only deduce that deep down he felt the same. He looked resigned. 'I can at least put out feelers for you.'

'Thanks.' Karen had no intention of taking him up on that offer, but was disinclined to throw it in his face right now. She might even consider returning home for a spell in order to re-evaluate her future. For the present, ambition appeared to be taking a back seat.

Jake and Howard returned triumphant some little time later. The jaguar had not only come down to drink, but brought a couple of cubs with her too. Howard ran the sequence back through the viewfinder for the rest of them. Watching, Karen could only wish she had been there on the spot.

Mike was studiously ignoring her this morning. It was apparent that he still felt himself the injured party. No matter what his misconceptions, there was no excuse for his behaviour, Karen told herself. She refused to feel guilty.

Where Jake was concerned she felt everything. She tried her best to steer clear of him, but in such a relatively small party that wasn't easy. Finding him following in her wake on the trail made her wonder if he was deliberately keeping an eye on her in case she acted on last night's impulse and took off on her own. She would have to be mad to even consider it. The trail itself was already growing faint; once away from it, and minus a compass, she would be lost within minutes.

'I'm not going to do anything silly,' she said at length, goaded beyond endurance by his silence. 'You've already convinced me. I'd as soon not have you at my back.'

'We need to talk,' he returned levelly.

Karen gave a derisive little laugh. 'What is there to talk about?'

'A number of things.'

'I was under the impression that we said everything there was to say last night.' She let the pause stand for a moment before adding, 'Or is that just the excuse?'

There was no alteration in tone. 'Excuse for what?'

'A reinstatement of liberties, perhaps? After all, we still have a long way to go. Why not make the most of it?'

Jake said softly, 'Is that the way you feel?'

She made haste to retract any false impression. 'I was simply outlining the kind of scenario a man like you might have in mind. I wouldn't let you near me again for a fortune!'

'I'm unlikely to be offering you money,' came the response, 'though I can't deny I still want you. You want me too. If there's one thing I *am* sure of, it's that.' He put his hand on her shoulder. 'Karen——'

They were the last in line; the rest of the party was already passing from sight. She yanked herself clear of his grasp, stumbled over a tree root as she moved too hastily away from him, and came down heavily on one knee. The pain made her feel sick for a moment. It brought involuntary tears to her eyes. She dashed them away with the back of her hand as Jake started forward to help her, pushing herself back to her feet with a jerky movement that almost made her cry out.

'Leave me alone!' she gritted through clenched teeth. 'I can manage!'

'Not from where I'm standing.' He caught hold of her as she attempted to walk. 'Just take it easy for a minute or two, will you?'

'It's just bruised, that's all. If I don't keep moving it's going to stiffen up.' She held her face rigid. 'We've already lost enough time.'

'That's the least concern. I'm prepared to take your word for it with regard to the bruising. I doubt if you'd be capable of standing at all if it were any worse.' He was supporting her now with an arm about her waist. 'All the same, you're going to need help for a while.'

'Not yours,' she flashed.

'You'd prefer Mike, perhaps?' His tone was dry. 'I could always call him back.'

He would do it, she knew. Refusing Jake's assistance on the grounds of personal feelings was stupid; she knew that too.

The arm about her waist tautened its grasp when she made no reply. 'All right, so let me take your weight.'

Karen did so, favouring the injured member, which was still radiating pain. It was going to stiffen up regardless once she stopped moving for any length of time, but that would have to be dealt with as and when. For the moment, just being this close to Jake again was enough to cope with.

The density of foliage far overhead cut out all but the occasional shaft of sunlight, creating a cathedral-like dimness. Undergrowth was sparse enough to make the going relatively easy. But for the ever-present background of sound, and the clinging humidity, they might have been in an English forest. Many of the trees themselves were familiar.

'We may as well take advantage of the privacy to get a few things straight,' said Jake after a moment or two. 'First and foremost, I am not about to become Elena's second husband. If that really was what she told Roger, then I have some straightening out to do with her too when we get back.'

Karen hardly knew what to think. The statement had come as a total surprise. She wanted to believe him, yet the doubt refused to be banished that easily. Why would Elena have said it if Jake hadn't given her good reason?

'You could have denied it last night,' she said huskily.

'I was in no mood last night to start denying anything,' he returned. 'Up there in the hide, while we were waiting for the cat to put in an appearance, I had time to think things through. I'm of the opinion that I might have jumped to a few too many conclusions myself. Taking any notice at all of what Mike had to say was my biggest mistake.'

'You mean you don't believe I encouraged him to think I was keen on him?'

'Meaning I don't believe you meant to give that impression—any more than you did with Roger. Your problem seems to be in failing to recognise the difference between sympathetic interest and serious involvement. Not that it excuses Mike's behaviour—or mine either.' The last on a wry note. 'I hope you'll give me more benefit of the doubt than I allowed you.'

Karen took her time digesting this new development. If Jake was telling the truth, then Elena had to be lying. Yet why should she be? And why to Roger, of all people?

'Considering what you think about my motives,' she said slowly and carefully, 'is it possible you might have given Elena the wrong impression yourself? After all, you and she are...were...'

'Lovers?' he supplied as she hesitated over the word. 'I'm not denying it. It was a mistake on my part. I'm not denying that either. If she read more into it than what was actually there, then I'm sorry, but marriage was certainly never mentioned.'

'You didn't...make love to her the night of the barbecue?'

'No, I didn't. It was over some time ago for me. I thought for her too.'

'But you still went when she called.'

'She said she had to talk to me about her brother—the one I was at university with. He was in trouble. It turned out to be something and nothing.' Jake paused. 'I realise now that she was simply fetching me away from you.'

'Why should she feel the need?'

'Because she could see I was attracted to you.'

'She must have been relieved to learn you'd no intention of taking me with you.' Karen still wasn't wholly convinced. 'I gather you did tell her that?'

'Yes. I really thought you wouldn't be able to take it. I didn't count on your stubbornness. Or, then again, maybe I did, subconsciously. In any case, I planned on looking you up after we got back.'

Luz appeared through the trees up ahead. His face cleared when he saw the two of them.

'We only discovered you weren't with us a few minutes ago,' he said. 'What happened?'

'I tripped,' Karen answered. 'Nothing serious. Just a bruised kneecap.'

'Enough to create problems once you stop moving. I know of a remedy, if I can find the plant I need. Can you manage,' he added to Jake, 'while I go to look for it? I'll have the others wait where they are.'

'We're doing fine,' Jake assured him. 'We can't be more than five minutes behind.'

'Closer to ten at the pace you're going.'

'Can you go on?' asked Jake as the other man faded back into the trees. 'Or do you want to rest for a minute or two?'

The pain in her knee was secondary to other matters right now, Karen acknowledged. Everything Jake had told her seemed to suggest a deeper regard than he had ever given her reason to hope for. Only wasn't it all just a little too pat? He still wanted her, he had admitted a little while ago, and she herself knew how vital that urge could be. Possibly enough so on his part to put aside all other considerations, if only for the duration of the journey.

'We'll go on,' she said. 'In fact, I can walk without help now, I think.'

'Try it,' he invited. He removed the supporting arm, mouth taking on an ironic little smile as she attempted to bring her full weight to bear on the injured member and drew in a sharp breath. 'Still want to be independent?'

She nodded, not about to admit that she couldn't take his touch any more and retain any sense of perspective. She needed time to think, to sort out her emotions. She had gone from one extreme to the other these last few days. Right now, she wasn't sure *what* she felt.

Jake allowed her to move on without help, although maintaining a close proximity. 'Stubbornness can be taken too far,' he growled softly. 'I've gone as far as *I'm* prepared to go without some kind of return from you.'

'What do you expect?' she asked.

'An attempt to meet me at least halfway. We had a whole lot going for us before we got at cross purposes.'

Especially in the physical sense, it was on the tip of her tongue to retort, but the words failed to materialise.

'So we were both mistaken,' she heard herself saying instead. 'Where does that leave us?'

'Right here.' Jake halted her limping progression with a hand on her arm, moving up and round to face her. The blue eyes held an expression to which she couldn't put a definite name: satisfaction; triumph; or something more far-reaching? 'It's the last bit of privacy we're going to be getting for some time,' he said, 'so let's use it.'

The kiss left nothing to be desired. Karen forgot her injury, forgot everything but the feel of his lips on hers, the secure strength of his arms about her. It seemed an age since he had last held her this way. Too long.

'I suppose we'd better make tracks,' he murmured at length with unconcealed reluctance. 'Otherwise we'll have Luz coming looking for us again.' He studied her face for a moment. 'No more misunderstandings?'

Karen closed her mind to the remaining doubts. 'No,' she agreed.

'Good.' Jake put an arm about her waist again as they began to move. 'So you won't object to this.'

They found the rest of the party awaiting them in a small clearing. Luz and Santino had gone to look for some plant or other, Roger advised. As it was close to noon, they had decided to eat lunch while they were waiting.

'Sorry to hold everyone up this way,' Karen apologised ruefully. 'Clumsy of me to trip.'

'It's surprising we haven't had more accidents of that nature,' comforted Roger. 'Lucky Jake was with you. I didn't even realise you weren't with us any more until Luz took a head-count.'

'Surprising we didn't hear you shouting at us to stop,' said Mike on a sarcastic note.

'Isn't it?' agreed Jake imperturbably. 'Anyway, no great harm done.'

'Are you going to be able to walk all right this afternoon?' Roger asked Karen, watching her gingerly stretch the injured limb. 'That looks painful.'

'I'll be fine,' she assured him with rather more confidence than she actually felt. There was some stiffness already, and it was going to get worse. A stick would help. There was certainly no shortage of material from which to cut one.

Luz and Santino returned with several large dark green leaves rather like the common dock in shape and texture. These were squeezed together until the sap oozed out, and then bound into place with a crêpe bandage from the first-aid kit. Karen did the bandaging herself, making sure she could still bend the knee. Whether it was wishful thinking or not, the pain seemed to lessen immediately.

By the time they were ready to move on, she found herself able to walk without too much difficulty, although the stick Luz had fashioned for her helped.

'This stuff is unbelievable!' she said. 'I can hardly feel anything.'

'It anaesthetises in addition to drawing out the bruising,' he returned. 'It may take several more applications. The jungle holds natural remedies for many ailments. Unfortunately, the plant I'd have needed to make medicine for Nigel wasn't to be found in that part of the forest.'

'Don't you ever get tired of this kind of life, Luz?' she queried curiously.

His shrug was non-committal. 'If I have need of a change I can always find it. The jungle satisfies most of my requirements.'

Karen changed tack, aware that she was unlikely to get a more detailed answer. 'You've known Jake for quite a long time, I believe.'

'Since he first came to Guatemala,' he agreed. 'He's a fine man. One I'd trust with my life.'

'How about your wife?'

'I have no wife.' Luz gave her a measured scrutiny. 'If you don't trust him why do you have anything to do with him?'

'I can't help myself,' she admitted.

'So you look to me for some assurance? I'm afraid I can't give you any. I know little of his life outside of his work. I don't need to know. You must decide for yourself what kind of man he is.'

Jake was talking with Roger and Howard a short distance away, making some point with a gesture of one lean brown hand. Viewing the hard-boned features, Karen wished she could only trust her own judgement. On the surface, he was all she could ask for, but what really lay beneath that well-controlled exterior?

They made camp as usual at around four-thirty close by the river. Karen took the opportunity to rinse one or two items of clothing through, hanging them to drip dry on a convenient branch. Jake came to do the same.

'One thing you can't get out here,' he commented lightly, 'is a well-pressed shirt. How's the knee feeling?'

'Fine,' Karen answered truthfully. 'Almost normal, in fact. Those leaves are magic!'

'You'll need to keep renewing them for a day or two, according to Luz. He's out looking for a new supply right now. Seems the fresher they are the more effective the result.'

'I appreciate his concern,' she said. 'Although I realise there's a measure of communal interest in it too, of course. We're running short on time.' She paused, trying to make her tone casual. 'Are you planning on coming back home along with the rest of us, or later?'

'The same time. There's the fill-in commentary still to record.'

'But that won't be until the editing is completed.'

'In which I'll be taking a hand. Plus, I do have other commitments.' Jake slung his own washing over a neighbouring branch. 'We'll need to move this under cover once it stops dripping in case of rain. We've been lucky so far. It's only come at night.'

Karen felt the tremoring response as he turned his head to study her. She met his gaze with veiled green eyes.

'I thought we were all sorted out,' he said in suddenly rougher tones. 'What else do I have to do or say to convince you I'm on the level?'

There was one sure way, came the fleeting thought, but he was unlikely to be offering *that* degree of commitment. He might well intend furthering the relationship after they got back to England, only there would still be no future in it. Better a clean break now than risk the kind of heartache any deeper involvement would certainly bring her.

'Nothing,' she said with resolution. 'It really isn't important.'

His brows drew together. 'That wasn't the impression you gave this morning.'

Her shrug was brief and dismissive. 'That was this morning. I've had time to think since then. I'm not denying I find you attractive, Jake.' She gave a light laugh. 'Even irresistible! I can hardly say otherwise, considering. Only that's as far as it goes on my side.'

'I see.' His expression was difficult to read. 'No reason why we shouldn't continue to indulge a mutual appetite, is there?'

'I don't think so.' Karen was hard put to it to keep her voice steady. 'It's over. Let's just leave it at that.'

His shrug was as dismissive as hers had been. 'As you like. Just so long as neither of us is under any illusions.'

She had never been that, thought Karen achingly as he moved away. Not even in her wildest moments.

CHAPTER TWELVE

APART from a little water in the bottom, the boats were safe and sound. As it was only midday, Karen would willingly have set sail for home right away, but the general consensus was that they left it until the following morning.

Considering the fact that they would be going against the current this time, it was going to take longer, in any case, she reckoned. The thought of a possible three more nights out here was dispiriting. And there was still Tikal to come after that.

All the same, her feelings when Roger announced his intention of using library film to show the restored Mayan city were mixed. Even if it did mean that much less time to be spent in Jake's company, it was unlikely that she would ever have another opportunity to visit the place.

There had been no personal exchange between the two of them whatsoever during the past couple of days. Jake didn't exactly ignore her, but his attitude was coolly professional. Often she found herself regretting her own attitude. What price future peace of mind at the cost of present fulfilment? Too late now, of course. Jake wasn't about to make any further overtures, and she couldn't bring herself to take the initiative for fear of what he might think. To all intents and purposes, they were finished.

Knowing it didn't stop her from yearning for him though. There were times when the longing became insupportable. Love took no account of circumstances. It couldn't be turned on and off like a tap. It wasn't going to be easy to get over him—if she ever did. One thing was certain: it would take a rare man to supplant him.

After almost two weeks in the jungle, none of them was either looking or feeling their best. Even Luz was showing signs of wear and tear. The lake was a temptation to most. It was only at Luz's insistence that bathing was totally banned. The piranha might not be in evidence, he said, but they were there all right.

Had anyone considered defying the ban, the idea was soon scotched by the demonstration he put on for that very purpose. The turkey carcass he threw in to the water attached to a length of rope was only there bare seconds before being attacked by a bubbling, seething mass. When he withdrew the carcase moments later only the breastbone was left intact, and that stripped bare of every last morsel of flesh.

Remembering the night she had been on the verge of taking a bath herself, Karen shuddered inwardly. If it hadn't been for Jake's intervention she might well have finished up the same way.

She could feel him looking at her now, and knew he was recalling the same incident. What had followed afterwards had been inevitable. If it hadn't happened then it would have happened some other time. It had been there between them from the very first moment of meeting. The antagonism itself had been a part of it.

'I don't know about anyone else,' he said, 'but I fancy fish for supper. How about taking one of the boats out and catching ourselves a few?'

'Of those things?' asked Nigel. 'No, thanks!'

'They actually make good eating,' Jake assured him. 'Although I had other varieties in mind. You've already proved yourself a dab hand with a rod and line. Want to try your luck with some carp?'

The younger man looked gratified. 'I don't mind having a go.'

Luz elected to accompany the two of them. Watching from the bank as they paddled out to the middle of the lake in order not to disturb the fish with the motor, Karen wished she had had the insouciance to suggest she went with them. The others were involved in technical discussion, to which she should be listening, but she still found it difficult to be anywhere near Mike without displaying her antipathy.

She was still sitting there on the fallen log when Nigel went overboard some time later. Exactly how it happened she couldn't be sure. One minute he was pulling in what promised to be a sizeable fish, the next he was struggling in the water.

His scream brought Jake to his feet. The dug-out rocked dangerously as he took a header into the water to surface at Nigel's side. Luz leaned over to grasp the younger man as he was forcibly propelled back to the boat's side, hoisting him on board with a strength born of necessity, then turning to assist Jake as the latter levered himself up.

From where she stood, hand to mouth, Karen could see several silvery objects falling away from his body. Alerted by the shouts, the other men had joined her. Howard was filming the scene with professional objectivity. Out on the lake, Luz started the outboard motor and headed for shore, and Karen came suddenly to life.

'Someone break out the first-aid kit,' she ordered. 'We're going to need antiseptic for starters.'

All three men had been bitten, although Luz's wounds were confined to the backs of his hands. Jake's shirt was in tatters, with blood seeping through in a dozen or more places. Nigel had caught the worst of it, though. Legs, arms and body were a mass of tiny gashes, none of them severe in itself but combining to create a blood-loss that looked appalling.

Karen had to forcibly remind herself that the human body could withstand the loss of a pint or more before it became a problem. She set to work to stem the flow as best as she was able. Shock was going to be the thing to watch out for, she realised. Despite the heat, Nigel was shivering uncontrollably, his face white as a sheet.

'My own fault,' he got out. 'I overbalanced.'

'You'll be all right,' Luz assured him. 'No major damage done. You must have cut yourself going in for the piranha to be attracted so swiftly.' He touched Karen's arm. 'The plant I used to stop the pain in your knee will work here too. I'll go and find some.'

More effective than aspirin, for sure, she thought. They had all had tetanus boosters before setting out, so at least that aspect was taken care of.

Having done all she could for Nigel for the moment, she turned her attention to Jake. He had taken off the ruined shirt, and the bleeding had almost stopped, but the wounds still needed tending. Karen steeled herself to touch the bronzed bare back presented to her without allowing the quivering inside to register through her fingers. The antiseptic must sting like fury, she knew, but he gave no indication as she pressed the soaked cotton wool over each laceration.

On her instruction, Roger and Mike helped Nigel over to his bed space and laid him down with his legs raised higher than his head. Luz returned bearing quantities of the dock-like leaf, which he immediately began crushing into a pulp in order to cover all the wounds.

'You should have some of that on yours too,' said Karen to Jake as she recapped the plastic bottle. 'They must hurt.'

'I've known worse,' he responded. 'We were lucky.'

'Not just luck. Nigel wouldn't have stood a chance if you hadn't gone in after him.' He was still sitting with his back to her, dark head shining in the sunlight. Karen resisted the urge to reach out and smooth her fingers over the exposed nape. That would be too much a give-away. 'It was the bravest thing I've ever seen!'

He turned then to look at her, a glimmer of a smile on his lips. 'Don't make me out any hero. I was acting on pure impulse. If I'd had time to think about it I'd probably have cried off.'

'No, you wouldn't.' Karen tried her best to make the statement matter-of-fact. 'You saved his life.'

The shrug was brief. 'He'd have got out on his own if he hadn't cut himself. That demo Luz gave was a bit tongue-in-cheek. They'll go for the scent of cooked meat, or blood, but, providing you don't have any open wounds, you're normally safe enough. Even then, it takes longer than the few seconds usually depicted to kill any-thing bigger than a monkey.'

'That wasn't what you told me when...' she began, breaking off abruptly as she realised what she had been about to say.

'So I exaggerated a little.' He sounded unrepentant. 'It was still a risk—or would you rather have taken that than what did happen?'

She should have known, Karen thought painfully, that he wouldn't allow the slip to pass without comment.

'I don't want to talk about it,' she said through stiff lips. 'It's over, Jake!'

'It doesn't have to be.'

'It does for me.'

Eyes narrowed, he said, 'You mean you've lost interest wholesale?'

'Is that so difficult to accept?'

'Considering the way we were, yes, it is.'

'Then you'll just have to take my word for it.'

Karen was nearing the end of her tether. The temptation to let the future take care of itself was almost overwhelming. Except that Jake was unlikely to be static for longer than a few weeks before setting out on yet another of his projects, she reminded herself.

She was going around in circles and getting nowhere, she acknowledged hollowly. Better to stick to her guns and call it a day.

'I'd better go and check on Nigel,' she said.

She left him sitting there, and walked unsteadily over to where the younger man was laid. His colour was beginning to return to normal, she noted in relief. Shock could be a killer in itself. Nigel greeted her with a wan smile.

'I seem to be fated,' he murmured. 'First the stomach bug, now this! I think I might opt for a studio job.' He managed a weak grin as she placed her fingers around his wrist to check his pulse rate. 'You'd better get one of the others to do that if you want a true reading.'

It was only the fact that he was injured that stopped Karen from coming back with a short and sharp reply to the sally. She had had enough of masculine responses along that same vein. Her own fault, of course. Jake had warned her of the probable consequences of being the only female in the party. Whatever job she took after this one, she would make darn sure she was never in the same position again.

The day moved swiftly towards sunset. By suppertime, Nigel was feeling well enough to eat a hearty meal. All of them turned in early for a first-light start. With luck, they might make it back to Fuentas by the evening of the second day, Luz had declared. Karen hoped he was right. The thought of even one more night in this fast becoming claustrophobic jungle was more than enough.

As on the previous time, she woke in the early hours. Also as on the previous time, she couldn't get back to sleep again. There was no sign of movement from the others when she finally gave up on the attempt and slid from under her net. She could at least cool herself down a little by splashing her face and arms at the lake.

Silvered by moonlight, the water looked as inviting as before. This time, however, she felt no temptation to take the plunge. Stripping off her perspiration-dampened pyjama top, she knelt to scoop up the liquid in cupped hands and run it over her upper body, relishing the comparative coolness. She would be soaked again within minutes of drying off, but for the moment it felt wonderful.

Ears tuned now to variations in the general night sounds of the jungle, she caught the faint snap of a twig, and whirled to confront the intruder. Jake loomed large

and menacing against the light filtering through the intervening brush from the fire.

'I thought you might have taken what I said earlier
too much at face value,' he claimed. 'It isn't worth the
risk.'

'I'd no intention of taking any,' Karen denied. 'So
you can rest easy. All I'm doing is cooling off.' She drew
in a steadying breath, aware of her quickened pulse rate
and quivering reaction. 'I'll be coming back in a minute
or two.'

'I'll wait for you,' he said.

'No!' She came up on her knees as he moved towards
her, arms folded protectively across her bare breasts. 'I
don't want you here, Jake!'

'It's a free jungle.' He towered over her, his face in
shadow, his body tensed. 'I'll go where I like and do
what I like!'

'Not with me you won't!'

His laugh came low and harsh. 'No, with you it's going
to be what we both like!'

She went rigid as he pulled her upright. The hands
pinning her arms to her sides were like steel. His mouth
was ruthless, forcing her lips to part, the thrust of his
tongue a rape in its own right. There was an anger in
him that frightened her, yet at the same time stirred an
answering fury. She found herself kissing him back—
hating him, loving him, wanting him, all at the same
time.

No word passed between them in the following tu-
multuous moments. It was like being caught up in a
storm. Karen abandoned herself to it blindly, not
thinking only feeling. The anger in them both turned to
a different kind of passion. She wrapped her limbs about

him as he drove into her, glorying in the pure possessive
power of him, matching him stroke for stroke through
to the final cataclysmic eruption.

Coming down to earth again was all the more painful
for the realisation of that abandonment. Jake could be
in no doubt now as to how she felt about him.

He made the first move, levering himself up and away
from her with a jerky force.

'Now we can call it over,' he gritted. 'Account closed!'

Not for her, she thought achingly. Not for a long time
to come!

After two weeks of nothing but jungle, lake and river,
Guatemala City seemed like another planet. Viewing the
suburban sprawl from the air, Karen wished they could
bypass the whole place and fly straight on home,
although, even if Roger hadn't plumped for a rest period
first, the chances of getting a flight right away would
have been remote, she supposed.

All of them were in dire need of rest and recuperation,
it had to be admitted—Nigel especially. Despite the attention given, one or two of his wounds had festered.
The first thing needed was hospital treatment. She would
be accompanying him there herself as soon as they
landed, leaving the rest of the party to make their way
to the house for the coveted hot shower and fresh
clothing.

The last two or three days had been the hardest of all
to get through. Jake had left her strictly alone. Seated
just across the aisle, head back against the rest and eyes
closed, he looked both untouched and untouchable. Not
that she had any intention of trying to reach him. There

was no point. He had had everything he wanted from her.

'I think Jake and Luz were the only ones to come through this thing unscathed,' remarked Nigel at her side, almost as if reading her mind.

'They were both bitten by the piranha,' Karen rejoined.

'I meant mentally. I feel as if I've been put through an emotional mincer myself.' He swung his head to look at her, expression wry. 'I got a bit carried away, didn't I?'

Karen lifted her shoulders. 'Not that I remember.'

'You're just being nice about it.' He added reflectively, 'A kind of jungle fever, I suppose you could call it. Everything seemed so much more intense in there.'

If it had been a fever she was still suffering from it, reflected Karen wryly. And would be for some time to come. Living in the same house as Jake over the coming day or two wasn't going to help very much either. She braced herself for the landing as the runway came into view through the side port.

Jake's decision to accompany the two of them to the hospital was received by Karen for one with mixed feelings. While true that neither she nor Nigel spoke Spanish to any great effect, it was surely also true that there would be English-speaking staff on duty.

'Maybe,' Jake agreed when she said as much. 'Then again, maybe not. We'll not take the chance. You could be there for hours otherwise.'

He certainly managed to smooth the path. Nigel was whisked away for treatment within minutes of their arrival at the busy city-centre hospital, ahead of others already in line.

Aware of aloofness in the lean features as the two of them waited, Karen could only hope that this wasn't going to take too long. To be on her own with Jake was the last thing she needed at the moment.

'You don't think they'll keep him in, do you?' she ventured at length, desperate for something—anything—to break the silence between them.

'He'd have to be at death's door for that,' came the reply. 'Facilities are stretched enough as it is.' He cast her a brief glance. 'Worried about him?'

'No more than I would be over anyone else in the same condition,' she responded, and saw the firm mouth take on an all too familiar line.

'Even me?'

'If you'd developed an infection, yes. Only you didn't, did you?'

'Seems I'm immune to most things.' The irony was still there. 'What's the plan of campaign after this?'

'The same as everyone else's, I expect. A couple of days to get over the rigours, then home.'

'I meant long term.'

Her throat closed up. 'I haven't decided yet. I may even opt for a complete change.'

'Doing what?'

'I haven't decided that either.' She made an effort to lighten her voice. 'How about you? What's next in line?'

Jake shrugged. 'I'm due to start a two-month lecturing tour in the States after Christmas. After that, I've been allocated a grant from the Lorriston Foundation to work on a dig in the Yucatán for a year.'

A programme that was going to leave little time for personal relationships, Karen reflected, just as she had suspected. She had done the right thing in pulling out.

The hurt would have been even greater later on. It also finally and completely settled the question of his marrying Elena. Under no circumstances could she see the lovely Guatemalan incarcerating herself in the wilds of the Yucatán peninsula for even a week, much less a year.

None of which made a scrap of difference to her present state of mind. That was something she simply had to live through.

Nigel was returned to them, looking somewhat sorry for himself. The treatment had been both messy and painful, it appeared. He was going to be scarred in places, though nowhere it really mattered, he hastened to add. Karen had the feeling that those scars would be borne with a certain amount of pride. Few people could claim to have been attacked by piranha and live to tell the tale.

The three of them got to the house to find the others relaxing on the balcony. Karen left them all together, and went to take the longed-for shower.

The flow of warm water brought some degree of rejuvenation, the feel of squeaky-clean hair even more. It was going to take a while to bring the latter back to tip-top condition after the ravages that sun and river-water had wrought, she concluded wryly, viewing herself in the mirror as she ran a comb through the damp strands. She could see the split ends from here!

Facially, she looked little different from the girl whom had stood in this same place just over two weeks ago. It was only inside that she felt so much older and worn. The white towel in which she had wrapped herself sarong-style enhanced the fading tan on her shoulders. There had been little enough opportunity to renew it so far this trip so she would take advantage of the next couple of days. They would be facing wintry November weather back home.

There was a knock on the door behind her. She went to open it, feeling a sense of *dé jà vu* when she saw Jake standing there. He was wearing a towelling robe, with little or nothing underneath, from the look of it. His jaw contracted as his eyes moved over her.

'I need some things,' he said. 'I'll clear them out altogether later.'

Karen stood back without a word to allow him access to the room. The towel began to slip as she moved; she caught it up, conscious of Jake's passing glance and the renewed compression about his mouth. If he thought she had let the towel slip deliberately he could think again!

She stayed where she was, holding open the door while he selected clothing for himself. If she allowed it to close he might well take that the wrong way too. She fought to keep her face totally expressionless when he turned.

'What are you afraid of?' he asked.'

'I'm not.' She said it without inflection. 'I'm just waiting to dress, that's all.'

The blue eyes were steady. 'It's still an hour or more to dinner.'

'So what?' This time her voice revealed a slight but noticeable tremor. 'Time enough for a drink before we eat.'

'Time enough for a whole lot of things,' he said.

Karen drew in a shaky breath, too well aware of the answering leap her heart had given. She wanted him badly, but it wasn't enough. 'I thought we'd agreed to call it quits?' she got out.

His smile was faint. 'I thought so too. Only it isn't that easy. Unlike you, I can't seem to find the "off" switch.'

If only he knew! Gazing at him, she was swept by overpowering emotion. She was being a fool, and she knew it, but it made no difference.

He read the answer in her eyes. Dropping the clothing he had taken from the wardrobe on a chair, he came over to take the door from her unresisting hand and close it, turning the key in the lock as he did so. Karen trembled as he drew her to him. She was going to give herself away this time, but it no longer seemed important. She loved this man to distraction. That was all that mattered at the moment.

The towel fell to the floor as he loosened the knot holding it. Still kissing her, he moved both hands slowly and caressingly down the length of her body, renewing his knowledge of it with a sensitivity that set her alight. There was no part of her that wasn't his to do as he liked with, no secret she could withhold from him. She murmured his name against his lips, feeling his response.

The belt of his robe yielded easily to her fingers. She gave an involuntary gasp as he pulled her close against him. Her hips moved slowly, sinuously, drawing a groan from his lips—a muttered exclamation. She buried her face in the wedge of dark hair, licking the salt from his skin, savouring the taste of him on her lips. There was so much she wanted to say that couldn't be said, but love could be expressed in other ways.

He lifted her in his arms, carrying her across to the bed to lay her down on top of the covers and slide down beside her, and cup her face in his hands as he kissed her long and deep. And she was kissing him back the same way, holding nothing in reserve. Letting go with such totality was wonderful, intoxicating; she couldn't give him enough of herself, couldn't have enough of him. She allowed both hands and mouth free expression, exploring every inch of that wonderful, hard-muscled body, feeling him tense, hearing him gasp, knowing herself for once in control. He was all vibrant male, pulsing beneath her caressing fingers, surging with power, with potency—the very essence of life. She opened her heart along with her body to take him in, loving his strength, his dominant masculinity. Jake Rothman, king among men!

'I'm not going to let you walk away from this!' he said low and fiercely some untold time later. His lips were at her breast, his weight still pinioning her. 'I want you with me, Karen.'

'Till the New Year?' Her voice was husky. 'I don't see the point.'

'So come with me to the States.'

She gave a brittle little laugh. 'The Yucatán too?'

He lifted his head, blue eyes revealing conflict. 'Are you asking me to turn the grant down?'

Karen swallowed on the sudden dryness in her throat. 'I wouldn't dream of asking any such thing.'

'Then there, too. It's an established dig, with proper accommodation laid on. No roughing it the way we've been doing this last couple of weeks.'

She looked at him with darkened eyes. 'What would I do there? Apart from provide you with home comforts, that is?'

'We could work together. You showed every sign of fascination with the calling at Chal Luz.'

'I'm not qualified,' she protested. 'I'd simply be a liability.'

'You don't have to be qualified to work on a dig, just intelligent and interested. You're both of those.' He brought up a hand to run a fingertip gently over her lips, eyes kindling at her involuntary tremor. 'Not on a par with the career you had in mind, I know.'

'It isn't that,' she denied, and knew she spoke the truth. Archaeological investigation was a career in itself, and one she found enticing enough to be tempted by the possibilities opened up. Only for how long? Picking up the threads of her life again later would be difficult.

'Then what?' he prompted. 'I realise it's asking a lot, but——'

'It wouldn't work out.' Karen forced the words through stiff lips. 'I'm not capable of living that way, Jake.'

He gave a wry shrug. 'I didn't think the trappings meant all that much to you.'

'I'm not talking about the living conditions,' she said. 'I mean the lack of long-term commitment. I know it's an accepted thing for two people to move in together these days without bothering about what might happen, but I need something more than that.'

'Such as love, for instance?' His tone was flat. 'It may be one-sided now, but it doesn't have to stay that way. At least give it a chance.'

'I can't.' She could hardly speak at all for the lump in her throat. 'I can't wait for something that might never happen.'

'I see.' He rolled away from her abruptly, to sit up and reach for the robe he had discarded. 'It doesn't leave a great deal to be said, then, does it?'

Nothing at all, thought Karen numbly. Her feelings for him went way beyond anything he felt for her. No matter how much he might want her, that was all it was.

She lay there gazing blindly at the ceiling until the door had closed behind him. She had done the right thing, she knew, but it wasn't making things any better. Two short weeks ago she had had her life mapped out. At the moment she couldn't even think a single day ahead.

Mike was out on the balcony alone when she emerged from the house some time later. She would have returned indoors if he hadn't put up a hand in silent appeal for her to remain. He looked uncomfortable but resolute.

'I've acted like a barbarian,' he declared wryly. 'I was jealous as hell and let it get out of hand. All I can say is sorry.'

Karen shrugged slender shoulders. The apology meant little to her because he meant little to her, but he was at least making some effort. 'Forget it.'

'I will if you will.' He indicated the drinks tray set out ready on a nearby table. 'Can I get you something?'

'I'll have a vodka and orange,' she said, deciding to let bygones be bygones. Settling down in one of the cane chairs, she added lightly, 'It feels almost cold here compared with Petan.'

Mike brought across the drinks he had poured, eyeing the thrust of her breasts against the thin cream silk with rather less detachment than Karen would have preferred. Leopards didn't change their spots, she reminded herself. Apology or no apology, he was still the same old Mike.

'Would you like something to put round your shoulders?' he asked.

She shook her head. 'I'm fine, thanks. It's only comparative.' She took a sip of her drink as he seated himself in the chair next to her, then replaced the glass on the low table. 'I wonder what's keeping the others?'

'If you mean Rothman, he went out,' came the reply made with just a tinge of malice. 'I saw him leave about fifteen minutes ago. Juan doesn't expect him back for dinner.'

He'd gone to Elena, thought Karen dully. He might not intend marrying the woman, but he had still gone to her. Her own fault. Had she agreed to his suggestion he would have stayed here with her. Only would she have felt any better if she had agreed?

The answer to that had to be that she couldn't possibly have felt worse than she did right now, knowing where he was and with whom. Mike wasn't the only one to be driven by jealousy of another. She was torn in two by it.

For her, the evening was long and tedious. She was thankful when the time came that she could announce her retirement for the night. Jake's absence had been accepted by the others without undue comment. He was, after all, free to do his own thing.

Tomorrow he was due to hand over the artefacts found at Chal Luz to the proper authority. Roger wanted the actual presentation on record, which meant the whole team going along. Once that was over, there was nothing to stop each and every one of them from following his or her own personal preference for the next couple of days. Karen wasn't sure what she would find to do with her time. Anything except mope around feeling sorry for herself, was her only plan so far.

As on other nights, she woke in the early hours, and was unable to get back to sleep again. Mind over-active, she gave up on the attempt in the end and got out of bed to go and find herself something to read. The moonlight was bright enough to make any extra light unnecessary until she reached the living-room, where she needed it to see the titles of the books shelved at the rear.

There were a number of English ones, she was glad to note, both fiction and non-fiction. She chose a Le Carré novel as the most likely to tax her mental processes to the point of sleep, almost dropping it when she turned to find Jake standing in the opened balcony doorway. He was wearing the same towelling robe he had worn earlier, his feet thrust into leather sandals. He looked weary, she thought in the timeless pause before he spoke.

'Having the same trouble?'

'If you mean not being able to sleep, yes,' she returned. Her voice sounded heavy in her ears; she made an attempt to lighten it. 'I thought a book might help.'

'Depends on the content,' he said. 'If it's good you might find it keeps you awake.'

'So what's your solution?' she asked, and wished she hadn't as she saw the strong mouth twist. She added hurriedly, 'Don't answer that.'

'I wasn't about to,' he said. 'Caffeine's hardly the right thing either, but I was coming in to make myself some coffee. Care to join me?'

Her better judgement told her to say her goodnight now and make her escape, but her better judgement wasn't in charge of her reflexes. She found herself moving to accompany him to the kitchen, the book still clutched in her hand. A cup of coffee wasn't going to change anything, for better or for worse. All it could do was prolong the moment of parting.

Jake used the smaller of the two cafetières, his movements quick and economical. Perched on one of the high bar-stools, Karen sipped at the aromatic black liquid and racked her brain for some impersonal topic of conversation. When she did speak it wasn't at all what she had meant to say.

'You went to see Elena, didn't you?'

His back half turned to her as he spooned sugar into his own cup, Jake nodded. 'Yes, I did.'

Having come this far, she thought fatalistically, why not go the whole way? 'With what conclusion?' she asked.

He leaned against the counter, cup in hand, expression difficult to read with any clarity. 'What conclusion would you prefer?'

'That's rather up to you.'

'Meaning you never really believed there was no arrangement between us.' It was a statement, not a question. He went on levelly, 'Elena denies ever telling Roger we were going to be married. She says he must have misunderstood her.'

Karen looked at him for a long indecisive moment. 'Do you think that's likely?'

The broad shoulders lifted in a brief shrug. 'If there was any misunderstanding at all, there isn't any longer.'

She said carefully, 'Meaning what?'

'Just what it says. I told her about us.'

Green eyes met blue, unable to penetrate the barrier. 'Everything?'

He shook his head. 'Not in detail, just in essence.' His mouth stretched to a cynical smile. 'I left out the one-sided aspect too. When it came to the push, my ego wouldn't let me admit to loving a woman who doesn't feel the same way about me.'

She must have misheard him, thought Karen, gazing at him blankly. He couldn't have said what she thought he had said. 'Would you repeat that?' she heard herself asking as if from a great distance.

The cynicism grew. 'Why bother? You made it all too obvious earlier that there was very little likelihood you'd ever care for me the same way. I accept it.'

She could still hardly believe it. How could he possibly not know the way things were with her? The same way she had failed to realise his true feelings, she supposed. They had both been so dense, so convinced. Even now, she found it difficult to say, although she knew it was there in her eyes for him to see if he looked.

He was looking too, but not with any great dawning of recognition. He said suddenly and roughly, 'No, dammit, I *don't* accept it! You can't just turn your back on everything we've shared these past weeks, Karen. I won't let you!'

He took the coffee-cup from her, putting it down along with his own on the counter, then reaching out to draw her off the stool into his arms. 'I can't get out of the lecture tour now, but I can still turn the grant down. There are plenty of others who'll be only too eager to step in. Come with me to America. Give me time to show you what it could be like.'

If there had been any doubt at all left in her mind his kiss banished it once and for all. It was so tender, so searching. She returned it honestly, sliding her arms about his neck to hold the proud dark head closer, cherishing his lips the way he was cherishing hers, heart full to overflowing.

'You see?' he said softly. 'It isn't going to be so difficult. All you have to do is think positively.'

'I love you.' The words came easily now. 'I've loved you for ages, Jake!'

He went very still, looking down at her with penetrating intensity. 'You haven't known me for ages,' he said on an odd note, and she laughed, pressing her lips to the strong brown column of his throat.

'Hours, days, weeks, it makes no difference. I was lost the moment we met!'

'Then we both were.' He was holding her as if he would never let her go. 'Why the devil didn't you tell me? Why did you let me think I was the only one?'

'Because I thought *I* was. Because I thought you only wanted me for... for...'

'For your body?' Jake was smiling, eyes glowing with a light she had never hoped to see there. 'That too, of course. And for this face,' smoothing it between his hands. 'And for your spirit and courage and sheer dogged perseverance. My life took a turn for the better the day you turned up here with Roger—even if I didn't fully appreciate the extent of it at the time. The real reason I tried to stop you from coming with us was because I hated the thought that you and Roger might get too close while we were out there. I wanted you to myself. *All* to myself.'

'I honestly never realised how Roger was feeling,' she said softly. 'Any more than I consciously encouraged Mike to act the way he did. It seems I'm particularly obtuse when it comes to reading people.'

'Only because you've no real concept of your own attraction. You fix those eyes of yours on a man and he's ready to believe anything!' Jake's laugh was low. 'I'll have to think up some kind of signal I can give you to let you know when you're doing it. Otherwise, you'll have the whole site team rocking on their heels.' He sobered again as he realised what he had said, mouth slanting ruefully. 'Forget that. I meant what I said about turning down the grant. What we really need is another project like this one, where we can combine our skills.'

'They're likely to be few and far between,' rejoined Karen practically. 'In any case, my particular skills could come in very useful in the Yucatán. You'll need someone to keep site records, for instance. I'm very good at organisation. I could become very involved in your work, Jake. As you said before, it fascinates me.'

The conflict was there in his eyes as he gazed at her. 'You sure about this?' he asked. 'You're not just saying it?'

She shook her head, loving him the more for his readiness to compromise. 'I'm not just saying it. Wholesale self-sacrifice wouldn't be any basis to build on.' She hesitated there, searching the lean features in suddenly resurfacing uncertainty. 'That's assuming we're going to be together for some time.'

'The rest of our lives, if I have anything to do with it,' came the steady reply. 'Do you think your parents would be too upset if we did them out of a grand ceremony and got married on the QT as soon as we can arrange it?' It was his turn to pause. 'That's assuming you're willing to marry me, of course. Not that *I'm* prepared to have it any other way,' he added with a swift and reassuring return to forcefulness before she could answer. 'I want you lock, stock and barrel, not on loan.'

'Me too.' She could say that with certitude. 'As to when...well, it's going to have to be quick if I'm coming with you to the States. Five weeks wouldn't be nearly long enough for Mom to arrange the kind of wedding she'd probably have in mind, so I think it might be fairer all round if we present them with a *fait accompli*.'

'What I was hoping you'd say.' He pulled her close again, holding her as if he would never let her go, face buried in her hair. 'I'm putting my mark on you, Karen Lewis,' he declared gruffly. 'I want every other man to know you're mine. We'll tell the others first thing in the morning.'

It was going to be a shock for them all, she reflected, but she didn't care. From now on it was her and Jake together.

'Let's go to bed,' he murmured, becoming the man she knew best. 'I've a whole lot more I want to say to you, my love.'

And she to him, she thought mistily. Words or actions, it all meant the same.

HARLEQUIN ◇ PRESENTS®

A Year
DOWN UNDER

In 1993, Harlequin Presents celebrates the land down
under. In June, let us take you to the Australian Outback,
in OUTBACK MAN by Miranda Lee,
Harlequin Presents #1562.

Surviving a plane crash in the Australian Outback is
surely enough trauma to endure. So why does Adrianna
have to be rescued by Bryce McLean, a man so gorgeous
that he turns all her cherished beliefs upside-down? But
the desert proves to be an intimate and seductive setting
and suddenly Adrianna's only realities are the red-hot
dust *and* Bryce....

Share the adventure—and the romance—
of A Year Down Under!

Available this month in
A YEAR DOWN UNDER

SECRET ADMIRER
by Susan Napier
Harlequin Presents #1554
Wherever Harlequin books are sold.

YDU-MY

Where do you find hot Texas nights, smooth Texas charm, and dangerously sexy cowboys?

WHITE LIGHTNING

by Sharon Brondos

Back a winner—Texas style!

Lynn McKinney knows Lightning is a winner and she is totally committed to his training, despite her feud with her investors. All she needs is time to prove she's right. But once business partner Dr. Sam Townsend arrives on the scene, Lynn realizes time is about to run out!

CRYSTAL CREEK reverberates with the exciting rhythm of Texas. Each story features the rugged individuals who live and love in the Lone Star State. And each one ends with the same invitation...

Y'ALL COME BACK...REAL SOON!

**Don't miss WHITE LIGHTNING by Sharon Brondos.
Available in June wherever Harlequin books are sold.**

If you missed #82513 *Deep in the Heart*, #82514 *Cowboys and Cabernet* or #82515 *Amarillo by Morning* and would like to order them, send your name, address, zip or postal code along with a check or money order for $3.99 for each book ordered (do not send cash), plus 75¢ ($1.00 in Canada) for postage and handling, payable to Harlequin Reader Service, to:

In the U.S.	In Canada
·3010 Walden Avenue	P.O. Box 609
P.O. Box 1325	Fort Erie, Ontario
Buffalo, NY 14269-1325	L2A 5X3

Please specify book title(s) with your order.
Canadian residents add applicable federal and provincial taxes.

CC-4

HARLEQUIN SUPERROMANCE®

HARLEQUIN SUPERROMANCE NOVELS WANTS TO INTRODUCE YOU TO A DARING NEW CONCEPT IN ROMANCE...

WOMEN WHO DARE!
Bright, bold, beautiful...
Brave and caring, strong and passionate...
They're women who know their own minds
and will dare anything...
for love!

One title per month in 1993, written by popular Superromance authors, will highlight our special heroines as they face unusual, challenging and sometimes dangerous situations.

Love blooms next month with:
#553 LATE BLOOMER by Peg Sutherland
Available in June wherever Harlequin Superromance novels are sold.

If you missed any of the Women Who Dare titles and would like to order them, send your name, address, zip or postal code along with a check or money order for $3.39 for each book ordered (do not send cash), plus 75¢ ($1.00 in Canada) for postage and handling, payable to Harlequin Reader Service, to:

In the U.S.	**In Canada**
3010 Walden Avenue	P.O. Box 609
P.O. Box 1325	Fort Erie, Ontario
Buffalo, NY 14269-1325	L2A 5X3

Please specify book title(s) with your order.
Canadian residents add applicable federal and provincial taxes.

WWD-JN

Harlequin is proud to present our best authors and their best books. Always the best for your reading pleasure!

Throughout 1993, Harlequin will bring you exciting books by some of the top names in contemporary romance!

In June, look for *Threats and Promises* by

BARBARA DELINSKY

The plan was to make her nervous....

Lauren Stevens was so preoccupied with her new looks and her new business that she really didn't notice a pattern to the peculiar "little incidents"—incidents that could eventually take her life. However, she did notice the sudden appearance of the attractive and interesting Matt Kruger who *claimed* to be a close friend of her dead brother....

Find out more in THREATS AND PROMISES . . . available wherever Harlequin books are sold.

BOB2

New York Times Bestselling Author

Sandra Brown

Tomorrow's Promise

**She cherished the memory
of love but was consumed
by a new passion too
fierce to ignore.**

For Keely Preston, the memory of her husband
Mark has been frozen in time since the day he was
listed as missing in action. And now, twelve years
later, twenty-six men listed as MIA have been
found.

Keely's torn between hope for Mark and despair
for herself. Because now, after all the years of
waiting, she has met another man!

**Don't miss TOMORROW'S PROMISE by
SANDRA BROWN.**

**Available in June wherever Harlequin
books are sold.**

TP

THREE UNFORGETTABLE HEROINES
THREE AWARD-WINNING AUTHORS

Untamed

MAVERICK HEARTS

A unique collection of historical short stories that
capture the spirit of America's last frontier.

HEATHER GRAHAM POZZESSERE—over 10 million copies
of her books in print worldwide
Lonesome Rider—The story of an Eastern widow and the
renegade half-breed who becomes her protector.

PATRICIA POTTER—an author whose books are consistently
Waldenbooks bestsellers
Against the Wind—Two people, battered by heartache, prove
that love can heal all.

JOAN JOHNSTON—award-winning Western historical author
with 17 books to her credit
One Simple Wish—A woman with a past discovers that
dreams really do come true.

Join us for an exciting journey West with
UNTAMED
Available in July, wherever Harlequin books are sold.

MAV93

HARLEQUIN PRESENTS®

Coming Next Month

#1561 STORMFIRE Helen Bianchin
Jake Hollingsworth is one of the most chillingly powerful men Lisette has ever had the misfortune to meet. He's made it clear to her that she just isn't his type—which suits her just fine. So why won't he leave her in peace?

#1562 OUTBACK MAN Miranda Lee
Surviving a plane crash in the Australian Outback is traumatic. Being rescued by Bryce McLean, a man so gorgeous that he turns all Adrianna's cherished beliefs upside-down, is pure hell!
Outback Man is the sixth title in the Harlequin Presents celebration of A Year Down Under.

#1563 TROUBLESHOOTER Diana Hamilton
It isn't Imogen's fault that Alex Devenko has jumped to entirely the wrong conclusion about her relationship with his father. But shouldn't she have set him straight immediately? After all, it doesn't take her long to realize that Alex is not a man she wants as an enemy....

#1564 JUNGLE ENCHANTMENT Patricia Wilson
Kip Forsythe's first sight of Natalie West doesn't convince him that she can research a documentary film about a dam in the African jungle. She's ill and hardly makes an efficient impression. But Natalie will do whatever it takes to make a success of the job—with or without Kip's approval!

#1565 ONCE BITTEN, TWICE SHY Robyn Donald
Simone is used to hiding her emotions behind a professional mask. But Angus Grey thinks he knows the sort of woman she really is. After all, aren't all models like the wife who betrayed him?

#1566 A TIME FOR LOVE Amanda Browning
What does a woman do when the man she loves rejects her and then her daughter is killed in a car accident? She denies the tragedy and...everything is fine. And when the man appears to tell her that her daughter isn't really dead, but that neither of them wants her, she goes into battle—for love.

HARLEQUIN® PRESENTS *plus*

#1559 THE JILTED BRIDEGROOM Carole Mortimer
Sarah's "holiday" in the south of France is turning out to be far from idyllic—at least until she meets famous investigative reporter Griff Morgan. He makes no secret of the fact he finds Sarah attractive, but can he possibly be serious about her when he's been jilted by another woman only days before?

#1560 SLEEPING PARTNERS Charlotte Lamb
Lauren knows Sam Hardy is a heartbreaker. That's why she ended their relationship—she didn't want to become Sam's next victim. And now she's engaged to a charming, attractive man. So why does she react so strongly when Sam comes back into her life?

Too close for comfort

When Professor Jake Rothman refused to allow Karen to accompany the all-male television documentary crew on what she knew could possibly be the most exciting expedition of her film career, her blood boiled! The fact that desire flowed between them like an electric current didn't help matters.

But Karen refused to sacrifice her career to some outdated macho notions. So when she defied orders and joined the crew deep in the Guatemalan jungle, no one doubted her determination. But now she had to meet the challenges of one of nature's most devastating forces...Jake Rothman.

HARLEQUIN PRESENTS®
The World's Bestselling Romance Series!

ISBN 0-373-11556-3

11556

0 65373 00289 1

PRINTED IN U.S.A.